Hero of Bullfrog Hill

By

Mike A. Marr, Sr.

© 2002 by Mike A. Marr, Sr. All rights reserved.

No part of this book may be reproduced, stored in a retrieval system, or transmitted by any means, electronic, mechanical, photocopying, recording, or otherwise, without written permission from the author.

ISBN: 1-4033-1828-X (e-book)
ISBN: 1-4033-1829-8 (Paperback)
ISBN: 1-4033-1830-1 (Dustjacket)

This book is printed on acid free paper.

1stBooks - rev. 06/12/02

CONTENTS

INTRODUCTION vii
YESTERDAYS ix

SECTION I

GROWING UP SOUTHERN..1
THE HERO OF BULLFROG HILL 3
BICYCLES FOREVER...6
LIGHTNING AND FISHING...9
LAKE WYLIE FOOTBALL 12
STOP THIEF 14
BEATING THE HEAT 17
NOT WITH MY DAUGHTER 20
LADIES IN THE BUSHES 22
THAT KITE WON'T FLY 24
ONE BUS IN THE DITCH 26
PLOWING UP TREASURES 29
BIG WHEELS KEEP ON TURNING 31
JUST TRIM THE EDGES 33
YO-YOS 35
LOST GHOSTS..37
POLK SALAD AND CREASY GREENS.....................................40
DEAR OLD BETHEL SCHOOL 42
BASEBALL MOMS 46
WHOLE LANGUAGE SPELLING BEE 48
SPACE HEROES 50
BOARD OF EDUCATION 52
REUNIONS 54
SOME FOLKS SHOULD NOT DRIVE..56
TOUGH TEACHERS...58
CAN'T YOU READ THE SIGNS? 61
WHAT TO READ? 63

SECTION II

SNAKES, YANKEES AND OTHER CRITTERS 65

CHICKENS	67
SPENSER WITH AN S	69
HOG KILLING TIME	71
SNAKES	74
HORSES, HOSES AND HOMELESS	77
SPIDERS AND OTHER CRITTERS	80
WHERE IS SPENSER?	83
SOMETHING IN THE WATER	85
SNAKES REVISITED	87
A LITTLE SOUTHERN READING	89
SOUTH-SPEAK	91
THEY TORE DOWN THE MUSTANG	93
SOUTHERN LEXICON	95
HOW THEY DID IT UP NORTH?	99
YANKEE SPIES	101
PREJUDICE	103
DON'T CALL AT SUPPERTIME	105
MORE SOUTHERNISMS	107

SECTION III

LIVING SOUTHERN STYLE	109
TO KILL A MOCKING BIRD	111
THANK YOU CAPTAIN LYLE	113
STRANGE DEPRESSIONS IN THE EARTH	116
OYSTERS AND SEAGRASS BASKETS	118
SHAGGING IN NEW BERN	120
MINT JULEPS	122
ON THE LAKE	124
GAMBLING ADDICTION	126
A LITTLE QUIET TIME	128
SHAG	130
MISTER DUCK	132
DEATH OF AN INSIDE SALESMAN	134
WAITING FOR GOD	136
AFFAIRS OF THE HEART	138
VACATION	140
HALLOWEEN STORY 2000	142
THE BEST CHRISTMAS	147

WHAT NO SANTA 149

Introduction

I have never been one to let facts cloud my memories. I can remember a lot of things that according to the facts never happened at all. I can remember coming home from the hospital after being born. My sister held me on her lap in Dad's old 1953 Ford pickup all the way from Gastonia, NC. Even though the facts bear out that I was born in York, SC in 1950 my memory remains intact.

An Introduction should tell you what a book is about. This book is about so many diverse subjects that it might be easier to start with a story that appeared in the Lake Wylie Magazine back in 1997. Most of the following were articles in that publication in a similar form. I started writing them way back in 1995 on a monthly basis. Some are true some half true and some are pure fabrication. It is up to you to determine which is which.

Yesterdays

My daughter-in-law is always asking me why I write about old things. She's been a member of the family since middle school, but only got her papers a few years back. She asks, "Why don't you ever put me in your stories?"

Ginger, for you, I will try to explain. You are. You will be for some time to come. I write mostly of things that aren't anymore, things that were and meant something to the people who knew them and used them, things that have been lost in the shuffle.

I write about old men playing set-back in a beer joint that has thirty years worth of empties in the back yard. Can you imagine all the stories those cans could tell about the people who drank them? Some were drunk for fun, some for thirst and some to forget someone or something or just to lose themselves for a while.

I write of roads intersecting other roads. Roads that meandered and curved and split all to Hell just a few miles ahead. Roads that carried the old men home after a day of cards. Roads that carried the same old men to their final resting places.

I write of young boys playing baseball and football and golf with dreams of turning pro, of swimming holes and skinny-dipping, of snows that seemed much deeper than they possibly could have been.

I write of a time when the pace was much slower, when people waved at each car that passed and knew the driver on a first name basis, when going to the store was an anticipated event, not something you do on the way home from work.

I try to recall the collective memories of a community and to put those memories on paper so they won't be lost when the community has completely slipped away.

I write of things that helped form my life and define who I am. Things that are slowly disappearing from the landscape and each loss takes a part of me with it.

I write of the past because I am afraid that when all of the past is gone, I will be gone, also. The preservation of old times and old ways is the preservation of myself.

You, however, are the future and someday, when we are both very old, we will sit and rock and remember the day you picked my son up for his first date and promptly drove over several mailboxes. We will recall how bored you were with beginner Shag lessons. We'll talk about the Honda with the broken headlight and tailgating at Clemson Hopefully, we will laugh about the night my granddaughter was born and how nervous Rob was.

That past however is not here, yet, so I will continue for now to write about the things and the times and the people that formed not only Lake Wylie but me as well.

SECTION I

GROWING UP SOUTHERN

Life in the South is a little different. Heroes are braver, Mothers are wiser, Daddies are smarter and Children are lucky to survive. As kids we rode bikes without helmets, we skated without pads, we swam without lifeguards and we played tackle football.

Mike A. Marr, Sr.

The Hero of Bullfrog Hill

This has been a long hard winter. The wind howled and the snow fell and the ice coated everything in sight. The good element about a winter like this is, it stimulates conversation between neighbors. People who normally just wave at each other are now sharing hot chocolate and snow cream and reminiscing about winters past. Remember the snows of '82, we built the snow Volkswagen and got in the local Newspaper. Then in '77, it piled up at least fourteen inches in the front yard. What year was that, remember, it snowed every Wednesday for four or five months, '65 or was it '63? Anyway, it just doesn't snow like it used to.

When we were kids, we headed for Bullfrog Hill as soon as the first flakes stuck to the ground. We took homemade sleds, trashcan lids, dishpans and anything else we thought might slide and through the woods and across the fields we went. There was no need to call around; everyone would show up sooner or later. After all, Bullfrog Hill was the only really dangerous place we were allowed to go and only because our parents didn't know how really dangerous it was. Sitting at the top, you could feel your heart beat faster as you looked down that sixty degree slope and planned your turn at the bottom two hundred feet below. You had to turn to avoid going into the creek. After so many years of sleds, carts, bicycles and even cardboard boxes, the turn had built up quite a bank on the left side. The creek itself was a tributary of Mill Creek and joined it at a point where Mill Creek was just five or six feet wide, but there was a swimming hole beyond the bank and it was deep enough to wet you from head to toe.

When I was twelve, one of my cousins came into possession of the most wonderful winter toy that has ever existed. He had a corner section from an old ESSO service station. It was two feet wide and four feet long and turned up about six inches on one end. The inside was some kind of metal and the outside was enameled porcelain, the slickest substance known to man. All we needed was snow.

My sister's family was at our house, when the first flake fell. I asked if I could go to Bullfrog Hill and Mama said "Yes, if you take Steve with you." Steve was my six-year-old nephew, he whined constantly, his nose ran continuously and he was scared of his own shadow, but there was no alternative. I took him with me. Halfway there, he was already crying because he couldn't keep up, so I put him on my old beat-up sled and pulled him the rest of the way.

When we finally got to the Hill, Randy and Chuck were there and had packed the snow with an old dishpan. The sleds were running good when Danny Wayne showed up with his masterpiece. Everyone gathered around and waited for him to make his run. He pulled his mismatched gloves up, adjusted his collar and tugged his toboggan down over his ears. It got real calm, the only sound was Steve sniffling occasionally, and then away he went like a bat out of Hell, at least 200 miles per hour. He barely made the curve and then completely cleared the creek at the narrow part and ended up in the open field on the other side. You could have heard us yelling two miles away it was fantastic.

Danny Wayne pulled the ESSO express back to the top and asked the one question we were all dreading, "Who's next?"

It got so quiet you could hear the snow falling through the trees. No one said a word. Then Billy said he heard his Momma calling and Randy said he would go, but his leg was hurting. Chuck and I were staring at each other, daring the other to speak, when we heard those words. "I'll do it"

We all turned to face Steve. He wiped his nose on his sleeve and pushed his cap back out of his eyes and said. "It's my turn, I haven't got to ride all day, I want to go." Everyone turned to me. I shook my head, "No, if anything happens to him, my sister will skin me alive."

Billy said "Come on, he hasn't had any fun"

"Yeah" said Randy "Let him go, it will be fun"

Chuck filled in " I was gonna go, but let him go before it gets too fast for him."

Before I could stop them, they had my charge loaded on that time bomb and were giving him instructions on how to handle the curve, how to bail out if it got too fast, and what to do if he started toward a tree. The next thing I knew he was gone. That trip put Danny's to shame. No one had ever gone down Bullfrog Hill that fast and no one had ever missed the turn that badly. He rode up the bank and flew fifteen in the air, right between two large Oaks and then disappeared from sight, crashing onward to the swimming hole below.

No one moved. No one spoke. No one breathed. We stayed like that for three full minutes, then as if a gun had fired, we tore off down the side of that hill like the Devil himself were after us. As we ran up the bank, we could hear splashing and I knew that my nephew had drowned and I could feel the skin being pulled from my naked body by my insane sister. I sat down and started crying, "OH Lord! Oh Dear Lord!"

Danny Wayne's voice brought me back "Are you Okay?"

Then I heard Steve, "Yeah, but help me get it out of the water, I want to go again"

Steve became a man that day and the rest of us had to ride that deathtrap to prove that we were men too.

It is strange what you'll remember; sitting by the fire as the snow piles up outside, strange, but also heartwarming. I think tomorrow, I'll visit a place I haven't been in years. Now, where did I put that sled?

Mike A. Marr, Sr.

Bicycles Forever

I have recently come into possession of a 27" twelve speed bicycle with racing seat and handlebars. There is also a kiddy seat mounted in back, I don't know why. When I got it, the tires were flat, the chain was locked up, the rims were rusted and the paint was scratched. I won't say where it came from; let's just say that one man's trash is another man's treasure. After adding 75 lbs. of air to each tire and then applying equal amounts of rust remover, sand paper, WD40, spray paint and elbow grease, the old girl looks pretty good and rides like a new one.

My first 27" cost a lot more and probably didn't last as long as this one will. People do learn to take care of things after a while.

I finally learned to ride when I was seven. I know that is kind of late for a country boy, but I had the same problem that Calvin has. I was sure that thing was going to kill me. The bike was a plain old boy's bicycle with 20" tires and I realize now, it had no intent towards me of any kind. My brothers and sisters used to push me around the yard on it and that suited me just fine, as long as they didn't turn loose. After a year of this, they grew tired of the novelty and one by one learned to refuse my request for a ride.

I really didn't care whether I ever learned to ride or not until a girl cousin came to visit. She was almost a year younger than I and treated that bike like it was a motorcycle. She went up the driveway, down the driveway, across the fields, into the barn and out through the hayloft. She made me sick. That summer, I conquered the bicycle.

My cousin, Randy had the longest driveway in the world. From Oakridge Road, it must have run two miles back to his house and straight as an arrow. He was older and worldlier than I was and always wanted to drag race. I didn't know anything about drag racing except that the first one to the finish line won. Randy had added some new twists, like trying to run your opponent off the road. We were going to race for pink slips, whatever that was, Randy would always explain things better after the fact.

We tore off down that drive as fast as 20" bikes would go, me in my lane and him in his. When I started pulling ahead, he came over and bumped me. The whole world slowed down, Randy's bike slid under mine, my tires riding on top of his tires, I just enjoyed the ride. It would have been nicer though if he hadn't been screaming so loudly. When we finally stopped, he was directly under me, blood on his knees, blood on his elbows, blood on his head, I thought he was dead. Aunt Stella picked gravel out of his backside for two hours. I never did find out what pink slips were.

I wore that old bike completely out in about three years, and then one Christmas, I woke up to the best present I ever got, a 24" Western Flyer. It was red, racing red; it had headlights, taillights, streamers, and whitewall tires, rear carrier and a chrome chain guard. It also had a generator that ran against the tire to supply power to the lights and siren and a wind driven speedometer, that went all the way up to fifty. It was the greatest bicycle ever built. I rode that bike everywhere, showing it off to all my friends. I just knew it could even outrun the law, if the occasion arose.

The newness only lasted a couple of years, everyone else had moved up to 26" bikes and I was having a hard time keeping up. Then one day, I saw it. It was at the Western Auto in Gastonia. It was a 27" twelve speed-racing bike and I had to have it.

Daddy said "That is not the kind of bicycle for riding in the country. It won't last six months."

I begged and pleaded and promised to be extra cautious, if he'd just let me get that bicycle. He finally gave in and said if I raised the money, he wouldn't say no. That was all I needed. I had a cow I had raised from a calf. Her name was Claudette and she was the prettiest cow you ever saw. The term "coweyes" was invented just to describe her. I sold her and bought that yellow bicycle. Daddy didn't say a word. For days, Daddy didn't say a word.

Back then roads were different. Instead of asphalt, they put down a layer of tar on top of a layer of gravel on top of a layer of tar and so on. In the summer, when it was real hot, all that tar came to the top to form a sticky gooey mess.

Just above Mill Creek Bridge was the best place in the world to leave a black mark. Leaving a black mark or burning rubber is done by putting your car in reverse, backing up at ten mph and then snatching it into first gear. Inertia causes the tires to spin. We didn't know about inertia, but we did know how to leave a black mark. Bob Mauney's old '53 Chevy pickup would leave one about fifty feet. Carl Harrison's Daddy's '64 Chevy would leave one longer than that but we never found out how far it would go, because Carl kept running into the ditch. We would all have to jump out and push it back on the road and Carl would have to go home, because his Daddy was going to kill him. I really don't think Mr. Harrison ever knew that car was a street rod.

You could also burn rubber with a bicycle if you knew how and my new 27" wonder bike was going to leave the world record. I watched as several others went tearing down the hill toward Mill Creek and locked their brakes at the slick spot. You had to be good to keep it straight and avoid spinning out. There were several nice runs, but I knew I could beat them. I started all the way back at the Gin and was in 11th gear when they all yelled "Now". I locked her down and slid and slid and slid. I had just passed the longest mark of the day, when the wheels buckled. I don't mean that they bent, I mean they doubled over. My bike was ruined, my pride was bruised and to add insult to injury, I had to carry the thing home on my back while listening to everyone carry-on about how great a black mark I had left. Then they laughed. I had no bike, I had no cow, I had no money for my cow and I had to listen to Daddy say "I told you so".

The more I think about that bike, the more I wonder about this new one. Anyone want to buy a bicycle?

Lightning and Fishing

Look closely at the skies and see God's holy wrath
Look closely for the streaks, which cut an awesome path
Listen for the rumble that fills each fretful ear
Listen to the voice of God, and tremble there in fear

Momentary blindness grabs you; first all's white, then black
Smell the ozone, feel the chill, until your sight comes back
Momentary deafness as no sound but thunder's heard
Sit and watch in awe and dare not speak a word

There's an old story about a fisherman who came home everyday with his boat full of fish. The local game warden heard about him and asked if he could go out with the man and see how he did it. The fisherman agreed and the next morning they headed out together. After running upstream a mile or so, the man stopped the boat, opened a cooler, removed a stick of dynamite, lit it and handed it to the game warden. The game warden said, "Don't you know this is illegal." The fisherman responded, "You going to talk or fish?"

There are also tales about people catching fish with an old crank telephone. You put the leads in the water crank the handle and the fish float to the surface to be picked up.

If these stories are true, why doesn't lightning kill fish? As many storms as we've had lately, Lake Wylie should be covered over with dead fish. I know the answer!

I don't fish much anymore. I think I got through fishing in 1962 or '63. My Mother worked second shift while Daddy worked first. That left the old man and me to fend for ourselves all afternoon. His idea of a good time was to head for the river and drown a few worms. The worms were dug by hand from under old pieces of plywood placed strategically around the barn. Every day, when I came home from school, he would be digging worms and I knew we were going fishing. We fished Mill Creek Bridge, The Old Rhyne Hole on Crowder's Creek and occasionally made it all the way to Allison. By the time I reached my tenth birthday, I had drowned more worms than anyone else my age and realized that I didn't really like to fish. That's when I learned to swim.

The splashing bothered Daddy and ran the fish away, so he quit taking me. The only fishing I did after that was with friends and cousins. We would usually go at night and see the sun come up the next morning. Some real good wrestling matches took place on the banks of that old river, and you haven't lived until you've been swimming on a moonless night. Sometimes, after a few dives, you would lose your sense of direction and the only way to find the shore was to catch a glimpse of a glowing cigarette on the bank. You would swim toward it and hear someone say "Listen, did you hear that bass flopping?" Realizing you were at the wrong camp, you swam the other way, quickly.

Night fishing required that you set a trotline before dark, and checked it two or three times during the evening. A trotline was stretched from one bank to the other and had set hooks spread along it. It had to be baited and the catch removed regularly. Sometimes you didn't want what you had caught. A snapping turtle can be a real problem, when you're swimming along with a feed sack full of fish in one hand. If he bit into you, everyone knew he wouldn't turn loose until the next thunderstorm. The solution was to cut him loose, hook and all and set another one.

Grappling was another way to fill your quota of fish. To grapple, you went along the bank in the water and reached into the washout holes under the trees. When the sun was beating down, catfish would go into those holes to cool off. By carefully running your hand along his back, you could find his fins, wrap your fingers behind them and pull him out without much trouble. The big problem with grappling was that some catfish were way too long and slender and didn't have fins. When you came upon one of these, you backed out real slowly. It usually took a while to calm down enough to reach into the next hole.

The best grappling in the world was on upper Crowder's Creek, near the big rock known as Rhyne's Hole. The big rock is at a bend in river and the water is always fast there. During a heavy rain, the level rises and the rock diverts some of it into a small lake located beside the river. Catfish used to walk on their fins across the isthmus between the lake and the main channel. This was long before anyone around here had ever heard of walking catfish. We just took it for granted.

One hot July afternoon, Bo, Heavy, Bean and I went grappling down at Rhyne's Hole and were catching fish to beat the band. Heavy was the first to notice the bad cloud coming up and said we needed to head back to the car. The car was parked about a mile away; the best grappling holes are not easy to get to. We were downstream from the big rock and on the opposite bank. The lightning started popping and the thunder rolling and we decided Heavy had had a good idea. Straight across from the rock was a silt bar, like a sandbar without the sand. Bo and I reached the bar and started swimming toward the rock across the channel. Heavy and Bean were just reaching the silt bar when lightning struck the water not two hundred feet away. They both screamed and jumped straight up in the air at exactly the same time. Bo and I were about ten feet from shore and felt nothing.

I learned my first lesson about grounding that day and also why lightning doesn't affect fish. I suppose if some catfish were out walking and lightning struck close by, it might cause them some discomfort, but without a direct hit, it probably wouldn't kill them. So, how do dynamite and crank telephones work? Your guess is as good as mine.

Mike A. Marr, Sr.

Lake Wylie Football

September is here and fall will soon be in the air. With spring, a young man's fancy turns to Love, but in autumn, a young man's fancy turns to FOOTBALL. We have already had the Jamboree for area High Schools, the Thrifty Car rental Kickoff Classic was a classic and the Pros are finally through with preseason. Let the games begin.

Football is almost a religion at our house. We never miss a High School game, whether the team is having a winning season or not. We also catch several College games during the year. Being a die-hard Dallas Cowboy, it may take a few years to get to a Panther's game, but I'm sure we will come around.

Football has been a tradition in Lake Wylie as long as I can remember. On Mauney Hill, we played every day after school. If Cousin Agnes was gone, we played tackle, if not the game was touch, two-hand of course, only wimps play one-hand touch or flag. Two-hand touch is a game of honor. If you are running the ball and I yell "Gotcha", then I believe I have tagged you with both hands. The honorable thing to do is admit that you were down. This has led to many arguments over the years as to whether or not both hands were used. Bob never had that problem. He was always bigger and stronger than the rest of us and when he tagged you, all you had to do was count the fingerprints on your back and you knew two hands had been used. These pickup games were usually called because someone's Mom yelled that Supper was ready or Randy got hurt. Sometimes both would happen and Randy would take his ball and go home.

When Wayne moved into the neighborhood, football changed forever. Suddenly there were rules that no one had ever heard of, like no rushing the passer. With a rule like that, a man could hold the ball all day while everyone else ran around trying to get open. When you finally got open, the quarterback was always looking at someone else. This lengthened the game considerably. We finally modified the rule to allow a rush after a ten Mississippi count.

Wayne also introduced sidelines. As I said before, we played honorable football. The boundaries were an old tree or a bush or telephone pole and everyone was on their honor to stay in bounds.

Wayne would get his Mother's flour sack and lay down lines just like the real thing. The only differences were the field wasn't flat and you had to look out for rocks and clotheslines. My nose is still crooked after catching a touchdown pass in Wayne's backyard only to be stopped by the clothesline. That day, I took my ball and went home.

One October afternoon, we gathered at Wayne's for a pickup game. The Potts boys were there, along with the Harrisons and the Mauneys, but we were one short of even teams. Jane, Wayne's older sister said, "I'll play if y'all don't hurt me." "Don't hurt me, what kind of football is that, don't hurt me." I mimicked. Having no choice, we let her play and of course I had to play against her. The ball was snapped and a screen pass was completed to my side. It was my responsibility to block downfield. With hands outstretched, I caught Jane square in the chest, a good block, she went down. She didn't however get back up and my hands felt all mushy where I had pushed her. That day, I learned one of the differences between girls and boys. I have been building on that knowledge ever since. The game was called due to bruised......breasts and Jane never played with us again. I felt real bad about that.

When there was no game in the neighborhood, Pogo and I would play a two-man version of football. You ran the ball all over the yard until your opponent caught and tackled you.

Pogo, being a full-blooded Redbone Hound was an exceptionally good football player. Every afternoon, as I got off the bus, he would be sitting there with that old rag of a football in his teeth, ready to rumble. Daddy often said "That old dog ain't worth a damn for anything but Football." I never argued with him, I just smiled and ran off playing with my best friend.

As I drive around lately, I don't see many kids playing ball anymore. Maybe times have changed, maybe parents have changed, and maybe dogs have changed too.

I sure miss Old Pogo.

Mike A. Marr, Sr.

Stop Thief

Last week, I went by the Post Office to pick up some stamps. I asked the nice lady behind the counter for two books. She said 'Would you like regular or Christmas?" I told her it didn't matter and she handed me one of each. I paid her $12.80 and left. Outside, I realized that she had actually given me three books of stamps.

The mind is a terrible thing, my first thought was to take the extra book back and tell her of her mistake Then, I thought "Wait, this is the Federal Government, would they even admit to a mistake." I wrestled with my dilemma for several minutes and after visiting the Revco, I returned the stamps. The same nice lady was still there and I said "I think you gave me too many books when I was here before."

"Thank you", she said "I would have felt that in my pocketbook at the end of the day". She took the little book of stamps and smiled a great smile. Several other people in line looked at me like I was an idiot, but I felt something good inside and walked away with a spring in my step.

I think God must test us sometimes and we never can tell which are those times. Giving stamps back to the Post Office was one thing, giving them back to an individual was something else altogether.

I have always known that I would have to work for a living, because I'm not smart enough to embezzle and I'm too nervous to steal. The idea, that stealing is wrong, was embedded very early in my makeup. Theft is one thing I don't understand. Maybe, if I were hungry enough or cold enough or just plain mean enough, I could take someone else's property but I never have been any of those things.

When I was three, my brother thought he had a dog, but he didn't. Ol' Rock belonged to me and everyone knew it. Rock was out of a litter that included Rattle and Ruff, long before Rock and Roll was invented, my parents were occasionally ahead of their time. Rock looked at the world as his oyster and everything in it was his for the taking, including Mr. Bill's cantaloupes and watermelons. Most people will tell you that a dog won't eat fruit, but Ol' Rock would slip into the truck garden and bring home a prize about every afternoon. As far as anyone could tell, he felt no remorse He'd break that cantaloupe open and suck out every little morsel. I assume he was wrong for doing it, but he was a dog and it is hard to teach dogs about property lines. Ronnie ended up paying for all those thefts, but Rock reaped the benefits.

Just over the state line in North Carolina there was a little country store run by the Leggett family. Joe was from Mississippi and everyone called the store 'Sippy Joe's. My family traded with 'Sippy Joe, he kept a charge book and on payday, Daddy would cash his check there and bring home whatever was left. Joe had a daughter named Janice and at five, I thought she was the most wonderful person in the world. She made me play dolls and house and dressup, but I didn't care as long as I got to be near her. She had an older brother, Milburn, who wasn't quite right. Milburn would burn old tire casings for the wire in them and then stretch that wire between homemade telephone poles. He even broke the tops of Coke bottles to make insulators. The fields behind their house looked like a main switching station for Maw Bell.

People were afraid of Milburn and told Joe that he should have him put away before he hurt someone, but Milburn wouldn't hurt a fly. I thought he was the smartest person in the world. After all, who else owned their own telephone company, built from scratch?

My first encounter with the theft bug happened at 'Sippy Joe's. On the shelf with the candy bars was a display with Cadbury Chocolate Covered Cookies. The picture on the wrapper was irresistible, all those cookies spread out on a tray. Maybe those cigarette ads are aimed at kids. The problem was the price, I could afford a nickel candy bar, but I couldn't quite raise twenty cents. For several days, I planned my crime. I watched as Joe moved around the store and I knew where he would have to be for me to get away clean. It was a warm day, but I wore my jacket with the big pockets. Daddy was my unknowing accomplice. It was payday and as Joe went in the back to get his books, I made my move. I slipped that little pack of Chocolate delights into my coat pocket, went out the door and got in the truck. Daddy took forever to finish his business and when he finally came out he said," I thought you were playing with Janice". I just shook my head; I was too scared to talk.

Mike A. Marr, Sr.

When we got home, I hid the package in the barn loft and didn't go back to it for at least a week. I kept waiting for the cops to come take me away. At last, I was home alone and I headed straight for my hidden treasure. I had decided to try to sneak them back on the shelf and clear my conscience. Something had beat me to it, all that was left was a picture and a small piece of tinfoil with a smudge of chocolate on it.

Sippy Joe is long gone and the family has moved away and I'm sure no one ever knew about the Great heist, but if I could find him today, I would still give him that twenty cents. Rock could get away with it, but for me, life is too short to carry such a heavy burden.

Beating the Heat

Remember last month, when everyone was complaining about the cool snap? There were all kinds of quips being passed around like "Sure was a short Summer" and "I think we'll drive up to the mountains this weekend and watch the leaves change" Well, it's over, it's hot, real hot and getting hotter every day. I, for one, don't want to hear any complaints from you people who were upset about the cool days in early June, because it's July now and August and September are still to come. So get used to being hot and hush.

The summer of '97 may end up as hot as the summer of '61. That's the year we River Rats didn't need to take a bath. Early each morning that summer, we climbed on our bikes, with rods in hand and headed for the river, usually Crowder's Creek landing or Mill Creek bridge. We were in and out of the water all day, so no dirt had a chance of sticking to us.

Before the new peninsula divided Crowder's Creek at the bridge, you could swim across from the dock to the other side, This swim, along with a dive from the bridge was a right of passage to manhood. Today, you could probably walk across and the dive would give you a terrible headache.

One day in July of '61, we all gathered at the dock on Crowder's Creek only to find that it had been taken over by fishermen, only they were fishing funny. They would drop their lines loaded with weight over the side of the dock and walk all the way around to the other side where they would pull them back up, then do the same thing again. We watched from the bank for a while and finally asked "What are you guys fishing for?"

"Joey kicked the lantern in the water last night and we're trying to hook it" one of them answered.

"I'll go get it for five dollars" I said.

They looked at me like I was crazy and the oldest one said, "Kid, that water is fifteen feet deep. You can't go down there."

Jerry asked, "Since you're not fishing, would you mind if we swim here?"

"Not at all" they answered, "But don't get tangled up in our lines."

Mike A. Marr, Sr.

The third dive proved to be successful, I came up with the lantern and we hung it under the dock until they left. We sold that lantern for ten dollars and split the profit four ways.

Salvaging is just one way to beat the heat, skiing is another. The Wooten girls lived on Mill Creek and their Daddy had the best ski boat on Lake Wylie. Snake was dating Judy at the time and I kind of hung around with 'Tricia. I always suspected that Snake dated her because of the boat, but he did eventually marry her and they are still married today, so I may have been wrong. Snake was a daredevil and would try anything. One day, we were out on the zipsled and he suggested that we both ride and try to stand up together. The takeoff was okay, we were on our knees and planing water. Jimmy was in front and stood up first he had the rope. The only thing for me to do was to climb up his shorts with him holding me. We had just gotten to a standing position when we hit the wake. I dropped to my knees and Snake disappeared. He had fallen in front of the sled and the only part above water was his legs, the sled trying to cut him in two. When the boat stopped, it took ten to fifteen minutes to get all the water out of him. We didn't try that trick again.

The Plylers lived in Belmont near the Hot Hole, they were Judy and Tricia's grandparents. A cookout was planned for Saturday afternoon and we decided to go by boat, Snake decided we would go by boat. Snake always skied on an El Diablo and I had a modified Dick Pope that I had stripped and encased in fiberglass, one slick ski.

This trip was a bit long to slalom so we skied doubles. Snake, always being the gentleman, offered me the banana skis, they were wider and would be easier to handle in the rough open channel. I didn't realize that I was being setup The River was full of boats and so choppy that I swear there were whitecaps out there. For those of you who don't ski, banana skis on choppy water are like walking barefoot down a gravel road, you feel every bump. When we finally arrived at the Plyler's dock, my legs were jelly. Snake, of course, wanted to ski back home, but Mr. Wooten, bless his heart, said he wanted to open the boat up going back and didn't have time to pick us up if we fell. I still have a warm feeling for that man.

Hero of Bullfrog Hill

Sailing is another way to cool down on a hot summer day Jimmy and I took off from the Wooten's dock in their Sunfish. I asked if he knew how to sail and of course he said "No Problem". He was right we caught the breeze and sailed effortlessly all the way to the mouth of Mill Creek. It was a fantastic voyage. The problem arose on the way back Jimmy couldn't tack. Alter two hours of fighting that durn boat, we lowered the sail and swam back with the Sunfish in tow.

So, you think it's hot, get out and do something on the River. Isn't it the main reason you live on Lake Wylie? Go skiing, go swimming, go sailing, and just don't come to me complaining about the heat.

Mike A. Marr, Sr.

Not With My Daughter

If you are inclined to watch a movie in Lake Wylie, you have several choices. There is Lake Wylie Video, there is Movies, and there are others I'm sure. There is not, however, a Cinema, a Theater, a Drive-in or any other type of structure that shows first run films on the big screen. You will have to go to Charlotte, Rock Hill or Gastonia to see the new releases and then you will pay an arm and a leg. The last time we went out to the movies, it cost $6.00 each to get in $2.50 for a large popcorn and another $2.50 for a medium drink to wash it down. That comes to a total of $22.00 and the movie wasn't worth it. Never mind that I also had to have Milk-Duds and Diane had a Snickers bar.

When we were dating, the only place to go was the Drive-in or Passion pit or whatever you called it when you were dating. You always got two movies and one cartoon and the price was cheaper than renting videotape is now. Bessemer City and Belmont were both a dollar a carload and believe me, we could load down a car on Saturday night. We usually brought our own popcorn and drinks and would set lawn chairs up in front of the car. Most guys that I grew up with have told me they got their first kiss in their parent's car at the Diane-29. Some even told me about adventuresome girls they had taken to the drive-in, but when I dated the same girls, I lost faith in their storiesDuring the Sixties, there were all kinds of "INS". There were sit-ins, there were Love-ins and there were walk-ins. Before a date with a girl I was trying to impress, I mentioned to her Mother that we were going to a Walk-in. After giving me a stern look, she and the girl disappeared for a few minutes and I could hear bits of a strong discussion coming from the other room. It seems that the Mother didn't approve of me and was sure that I was some kind of activist trying to get her daughter in trouble. I'm not sure she ever did trust me after that. From then on, we just went to the movies, whether it was a Drive-in or Walk-in was not brought up.

My first real job was at the Sunset Theater in Gastonia. I ran the concession stand. Later, the Sunset became the place for young boys to go and learn about life. The raciest film, I ever saw while working there was *Night of the Iguana*. My first run-in with authority was at the Sunset, also. My boss told me to clean the bathrooms and after one look, I put in my resignation. Little did I know that I would spend the rest of my life in the Wastewater Treatment Industry?

As a young man growing up in Lake Wylie, one of the best things in life was slipping into the movies. Bob had a '55 Chevy with a pop out rear *seat*. We would load up the trunk with as many people as we could get and quietly go through the admission kiosk. After parking, we would push the back seat forward and crawl out, first one into the front seat floorboard, second into the front seat and so on, until the car was full. As I mentioned, the Sunset became the place to go and was the easiest to slip into. There was a dirt road that ran parallel to the entrance, we would drop off all the passengers on the dirt road and one would pay admission. Driving slowly down the entranceway, we would all climb in through the passenger door, having taped the interior light button before leaving home. The movies we saw would be considered tame by today's standards, but back then they were worth the risk.

All the old Theaters are gone now, the drive-ins and the walk-ins and the only thing left are the multiplex Cinemas with their surround sound. I wonder what kids do today when they date, maybe they just go to the Mall and wander around.

Mike A. Marr, Sr.

Ladies in the Bushes

As the days get colder and the television shows pictures of blizzards in the Midwest, I can't help thinking about swimming holes. Those hot sticky days when someone comes by and says, "Hey, let's go to the Rhyne Hole' or "We're going to Mill Creek, want to come?"

One very hot August, very long ago, Carl, Steve and Wayne came to the house on their way to the old swimming hole across from Wayne's house. I had chores to do, but they could wait and off we went.

The creek was roughly one mile from the main road and ran beside a big pond the same pond that Steve had almost drowned in, last winter, while trying to skate. You shouldn't try skating in upstate South Carolina, no matter how thick the ice appears. Although the pond covered several acres, it was only three feet deep, but when Steve broke through the ice, he panicked and started thrashing. The rest of us held hands and were able to reach him with a tree branch. Once, we had him clear of the water, we stripped off his clothes and shared our extra layers. We built a fire and dried everything, then headed for home, swearing not to tell. If Dorothy or Carroll ever read this he may still get a whipping, along with the rest of us.

We walked down the old roadbed, laughing and telling jokes and generally cutting up as young boys will do on a hot Summer day, talking about girls and cars and anything else that came to mind. We didn't have a care in the World. Except Wayne, he always called me Hood and kept saying "Hood, we have to be back by three o'clock, we're going to my aunt's in Spartanburg". The rest of us ignored him, since it was only One, we knew we would be back in plenty of time. When we got to the Creek, Bobby and Billy and a few others were already there and started choosing sides for battle as we stripped off.

It still amazes me, how fast time goes when you're having fun. We played Sharks off the Wall, and tag and who can hold their breath the longest and Olympic diving. The water was cool and the Sun was sinking slowly into the West, when we heard the snickers. Bobby heard it first and told everyone to shut up We all listened, but heard nothing. Someone yelled, "You're crazy" and pushed Bob underwater. This of course started another bout of water war and another hour slipped away.

We all heard Jane at the same time, "Wayne, Wayne, are you down here?" Nine boys dove into the water at the same time to cover their nakedness. Wayne, being the jokester, yelled back "Yea, come on down, we're just swimming". Nine boys came out of the water at the same time grabbing clothes and jerking them on.

Jane and her friend topped the little rise and looked down at nine half dressed savages and her brother who never swam nude anyway. They both had a twinkle in their eyes that said they knew something that we didn't know. Jane tried to act the big sister and said "Wayne, you were supposed to be home by Three. Daddy's mad as he can be." You could see that she was having a hard time not laughing out loud. Her friend just grinned and looked from embarrassed face to embarrassed face.

We never mentioned getting caught naked by a girl, but were much more careful from then on about how we swam. I guess we could have asked them to join us, but at that age, it was much better to talk about girls than to actually do anything about them.

I haven't been skinny dipping in a long time and wonder if that has anything to do with the fact that I'm feeling older. Maybe, next summer, when the Sun is high and the days are long and lazy, I'll slip off to the old swimming hole and cool off. I'm still not sure what I'd do if Jane and her friend come looking for Wayne again.

Mike A. Marr, Sr.

That Kite Won't Fly

It has been a long and wet winter, but hope is just over the horizon, With the winds of March, the drying out phase begins. All the rains settle into the ground and help form tiny buds on the trees and flowers. All the grouchiness of winter leaves our bodies and we, too start feeling alive again. March is like the day after the Grinch stole Christmas, the little Whos are everywhere singing and playing and jumping, completely oblivious to the fact that they have just been robbed of something dear to them. Some of those Whos are even flying kites. I Hate kites.

When I was growing up, we built our own kites from crossed sticks, some string, an old Newspaper and homemade paste. My family will tell you that I am something of a perfectionist. I can't even play Pictionary without getting caught up in whatever I am supposed to be drawing, and that trait always showed up in my kites. I built beautiful kites, I painted the paper and drew Dragons and birds and planes that I just knew would soar through the skies. There was only one problem. I wasn't very good at kite flying. They either never got off the ground or when they did a tree or power line would eat them, three days work gone in twenty seconds.

All my cousins could fly kites, Chuck had one that stayed up for three days and nights. He would send notes up to it by placing them on the end of the string and watching the air currents carry them up into the sky. Randy once used every piece of string in the neighborhood to attach to his kite. You could just barely make it out as a black dot way off in the distance. When the string finally broke, we assumed it landed somewhere on the far side of Charlotte.

Kids don't fly kites like they used to. Oh, sure, everyone flies a kite at the beach but then even I can fly a kite at the beach. One reason may be their parents have never had much luck at kite flying and have never introduced their kids to this art form. I know my brother-in-law tried to teach his kids.

They were all in the field above the house and the winds were just right for a day of kite flying. Tommy gave last minute instructions to Cynthia, who was the designated kite holder, "Just hold it on both sides right above the tail". He then turned and ran as hard as he could across the field. He could feel the string becoming tighter and tighter as he imagined the kite soaring to great heights. After several hundred yards, he turned back to the kite and the smile melted from his face. There was Cynthia only a short distance behind him still holding the kite on both sides right above the tail. He never said a word as he handed the string to Jesse and slowly walked back to the house.My Mother was my designated kite holder and even though we didn't have much fun flying kites, we did spend some quality time together trying. She was also my pitcher for baseball practice, but she never could seem to hit my bat with the ball. I still blame her for my failure as a baseball player. If she had only had a better aim, I would now be in the Baseball Hall of Fame.

March is just around the corner and it is time to get out and clean up the garden, wash the car, polish up the Golf clubs and start thinking about Vacation. If March were the first of the year, I might even be able to keep some of my resolutions. It is, after all, a time for new beginnings. The only thing I would ask of you as March nears is teach your kids to build their own kites and then show them how to fly them. You may be surprised at who has the most fun.

Mike A. Marr, Sr.

One Bus in the Ditch

It has rained at my house, every day since Christmas. I know the weatherman has said that the sun is shining, but I have lost all faith in him and his predictions. I planted several tulips on Christmas day and they are beginning to stick their little heads up, but I don't think it has anything to do with germination, I think they are trying to keep from drowning. I also moved some shrubs and am thankful for the rain that will help them acclimate but I wish the ground was hard enough to allow them to stand up.

Rain has always been a part of living in the Lake Wylie area. I live on Oakridge Road where I was born and raised and remember when it was only a dirt road. In the winter of '58 the rain was so bad the road became a quagmire (I have always wanted to use that word) and was close to impassable. The bus ran anyway, as School must go on and in front of Carroll Harrison's house we went into the ditch. There were many reactions ranging form cheers to tears. The younger riders were yelling and screaming that there would be no school today and some of the older girls were crying because we might have been killed. I really think they were crying because they wouldn't get to see their boyfriends. The driver walked over to the Harrison's house and called the school. For several hours we waited for a replacement bus.

When it finally arrived, the cheering died down and everyone quietly changed buses ruining shoes in the process. Soon we were all seated and the new driver pulled away. The bus slipped and slid past the hulk of the now half-buried bus and the rear end started moving toward the ditch on the other side. With a little help from the kids swinging and swaying in the back seats, there wasn't much the driver could do to prevent a second catastrophe. Soon, that bus too was stuck up to its axle. We all walked home and enjoyed a rainy day with no school.

Mr. Charley Neal came to see my parents shortly after they moved here. Dad had been a miner and was unloading several pair of rubber boots when Mr. Charley said, "You won't be needing those here, it don't never rain that much". A few weeks later, he was back asking to buy a pair of those fine rubber boots. Mr. Charley had a way of knowing how to find what he needed.

Hero of Bullfrog Hill

When we were growing up, we didn't have radar and Accuweather and early warning systems to tell us when the rains were coming, we had Cloudy McClean on Channel 3 who got the weather right about once a month. He once predicted that the next day would be partly cloudy; people were shoveling three inches of partly cloudy off their porches the following morning.

As kids, we loved the rain; it meant that Bull Frog Hill would be slick and fun was in the air. Bull Frog Hill is a clay bank that slopes off to the creek below. It was much higher when we were young, probably fifty feet or so. We took a lot of pains to keep it clear of roots and rocks and other debris and on a wet rainy day you could slide forever. The secret to sliding was a good cardboard box. It acted like a motor grader and plowed a path form the top of the hill to the bottom. After two or three trips, the box was so wet it became useless and inventiveness set in. Some would slide standing up like a surfer and making it all the way to the creek always brought a round of cheers. Others, after trying the surfing technique and failing would lie face down in the mud and bellyslide. Needless to say, by the end of the day, we realized that we were in trouble with our moms and would probably be beaten to death for getting so muddy. That's when the excuses started. Danny Wayne was always to blame, he either pushed us down or hooked us to his bicycle and pulled us through the mud or throw us in the creek or something. All the Moms knew he was a bad influence and may have believed some of the excuses, until washday when they had to clean the mud out of our drawers.

I grew up in the Old Oakridge School house that had a tin roof. My bedroom was upstairs and steeping under that roof during a rainstorm is one of my fondest memories. It was so loud you couldn't carry on a conversation, but the rhythm would put you out like a light. I have threatened to put a tin roof on our house when I have trouble sleeping. The attic of that old house was another good place to play during the rain. There were clothes form the '30s and '40s up there and just guessing what some of them were would keep me busy for hours. I also found some of my Dad's old books. There was *Old Yeller, Pilgrim's Progress* and *Lad, a Dog*. A stack of old magazines dating back to the late '40s was also there. I guess I owe my love of reading to those rainy days spent in that attic.

Mike A. Marr, Sr.

    As I look out, it is still raining, so I think I will grab a good book and curl up on the couch Rain can be enjoyable if you know how to look at it.

Plowing up Treasures

Have you looked outside, recently? That big bright orange thing that shows up in the sky, every other day or so, is the Sun. Now, I realize the thing is 93,000,000 miles away, but it sure is good to see it again. At my house, we are slowly but surely coming out of hibernation and enjoying the great outdoors, once more. We are even planting a few flowers around the place and some of them may live, if I can keep the dogs out of the beds. Why will a dog curl up in the middle of fresh pine needles, when he won't go near his house after you've spent time and money to put fresh bedding in it? I guess I never will understand the mental workings of a canine mind.

Another thing you are beginning to see, is freshly turned earth. The farmers are getting ready to plant their summer crops. If there is a better smell than a freshly plowed field, it would have to be something you can eat. I used to walk behind Daddy as he turned the ground and was often amazed at what turned up. I had a nice collection of arrowheads, but that disappeared along with my comic books and other collectibles. All young boys should follow a tractor at least once in their lives, the feel of the dirt between your toes is something that can't be explained.

Growing up, we lived on forty or so acres and most of it was either pasture or farm land, so each Spring, it had to be turned under and then disked. The turning plow usually brought the arrowheads to the surface along with everything else that had been thrown into the field during the winter. You would find the occasional baseball, usually just a core wrapped in electrical tape, coffee cans, I'm not sure how they got there and baby rabbits.

One spring, Danny Wayne had a squirrel named Rocky, all squirrels were named Rocky even before Rocky and Bullwinkle, and Chuck wanted a wild pet for himself. Daddy was plowing the big field and Chuck fell in behind him in hopes he would stir up a rabbit. Sure enough, after only a few laps, the little rodents scattered in every direction. Chuck pounced on the closest one and was immediately surprised at the sharpness of its teeth. He was also surprised at the length of its tail. He had caught a field rat, or maybe I should say a field rat caught him. The rat bit all the way through his finger and he was trying desperately not to hold onto the thing anymore. After much screaming and gnashing of teeth, Daddy stopped the tractor and choked the rat until it finally let go Chuck wore a bandage for several weeks after that and he never did get his baby rabbit.One Spring afternoon, I got off the school bus and had a religious experience. There, at the end of one of the rows of young corn, sat a three foot tall Buddha. I carried it into the house and was very proud of my find. I even did some research on Buddhism and learned quite a bit. The Buddha remained a mystery for sometime and everyone came to see it. Finally, Floyd Johnson admitted that he had left it there after borrowing Daddy's disk harrow. He had bought it at a flea market and there wasn't room for it and the plow on his truck. He never did come back to claim it though.

There was also the story of the farmer in Gaston County, who dug up an alien. The papers ran the story under the headline *Devil's Child or Hoax.* People wanted to believe the thing was part of some Kind of Devil Worship group, but we knew about Roswell and we knew that aliens were watching us. It only made sense that one of them would eventually die and have to be buried. The aliens couldn't possibly know that they had buried him in the middle of a cornfield. The official report stated that the object was a wooden mannequin left behind by the carnival people, but we all know how the Government hides things.

I'm getting all these ads for Troy-bilt tillers in the mail and I may break down and buy one this year. I can hardly wait to see what treasures turn up.

Big Wheels Keep on Turning

My Daddy had always worked in the "Mill". I know that he had done other things, like single-handedly building the Georgetown Bridge, digging for Gold in Charlotte and many other jobs. After I was born, he worked in the "Mill". This position gave him access to wonderful items for a young boy, broken cogs. The cogs were about a foot across and had rows of teeth that rolled in a rack. When a tooth broke out, the cog was useless and Daddy brought it home. They made great Go-cart wheels.

Transportation for a youngster in early Lake Wylie was very important and everyone had their own way of doing things. Randy's go-carts utilized old lawn mower wheels, mine had cogs. You could hear it rumble along for miles as the big wheels crushed gravel. It would also fly down Bull Frog Hill. The go-carts were built from whatever old lumber we could scavenge and nails that had been used and pulled and straightened so many times they looked like a librarian's index finger. A piece of short rope was nailed to both sides of the front axle to allow for steering and one large nail or a bolt if you were lucky held the axle in place. Some of these contraptions would have made the "Little Rascals" proud.

One summer, Maxie, Mickey and I were putting the ultimate go-cart together down by the old spring. We had confiscated some lumber, had a tin can full of various nails and borrowed Daddy's hand saw. The measurements were precise, you cut a piece of wood and if it didn't fit, you cut it again. Maxie was sawing against the old stump so fast and furiously that Mickey and I both thought we heard a motor. We told him to stop for a second and the buzzing stopped with him. We couldn't make out the sound but it was familiar. Maxie started sawing again and the motor sound started too. After three or four sawing sessions, the yellow jackets stopped warning and came after us in earnest. You have never seen three kids run that fast and strip clothes at the same time. By the time we reached the house, we were down to our shorts and had very few places that weren't stung. I missed a trip to Love Valley that weekend but it was all right my eyes were swelled shut and I couldn't have seen the bull riders anyway.

Mike A. Marr, Sr.

    Another method of transportation was the horse drawn sled. We all heated with wood stoves and someone had to gather the firewood. A sled was just two 2x4s cut at an angle for runners and various boards nailed to the top of them for a platform. Riding the sled was one of the great pleasures of growing up in the country. Charlie Horse would plod along at his own pace regardless of what you wanted him to do and the sled would tag along behind him. The woods behind our house were full of sledding trails and Daddy and I would cut the firewood and stack it beside these trails.

    Later, Charlie and I would go back and load the wood. A horse can become a close friend if you spend the day with him gathering firewood. We would be pirates on the open sea for awhile and then we would play Santa delivering presents. The games were the only way to keep your sanity. I think Charlie enjoyed them as much as I did.

Just Trim the Edges

What is the deal with hair these days? Every time you turn on the television there is a commercial about hair. One has a man looking in the mirror and his reflection has less hair than he does. Another one is about removing hair from all the places it shouldn't grow; women are in this one. It seems to me that there have to be more important issues around than the hair on our heads and body.

Hair is one those strange things that definitely has a place. There is nothing so sensuous as a lady's hair falling across your face as you embrace her. You bury your nose in it and sometimes even nibble at it. Some young girls even chew their own hair when they are lost in concentration. All those strands of glorious hair are delicious until one of them comes loose and ends up in your mashed potatoes. The same hair that you cherished just moments before is now the most disgusting thing in the universe. A hair in your food is almost as bad as some old degenerate blowing his nose at the next table.

As a young boy, I remember going to the barbershop every Saturday morning to get a trim. There was nothing much to trim however since we all wore our hair so short that the barber spent most of his time clicking his scissors in the air so it sounded like he was actually doing something. The best part was when he splashed that foo foo juice on your neck and the scent followed you the rest of the day.

There was a story about a preacher who told the barber not to put any of that stuff on him because his wife would think he had been in a French Bordello. The man in the next chair said "Give me his share, my wife doesn't know what one of those places smells like" The preacher left in a huff. Women in those days wore their hair long, usually down to the shoulders or longer. That way you could tell the difference between the sexes a mile away. My mother wore his in plaits or in a French bun and I never knew how long her hair actually was. Most of the women I knew were the same way, they wore buns and plaits and beehives more commonly known as big hair. Did I tell you about the lady who wore her hair up so long that mice built a nest in her beehive? I didn't know her personally but she was the aunt of one my best friend's cousin's husband's friends so I know that it was true.

The Beatles put an end to all that hair differentiation. Teenage boys started letting their hair grow long in defiance of their parents. They were so radical in those days that I seem to remember that some of those long hairs even chewed gum in class.

I joined this antiestablishment movement in the seventh grade and stopped going to the barber every week. Of course I stopped a lot of things in the seventh grade. I wasn't rebellious, I was just lazy and this looked like a perfect opportunity to sleep late on the weekend. I did however get tagged with all kinds of labels; hippie, hood and longhaired freak come to mind.

There was a War movie about women who were captured in Germany. I don't remember the name of the movie but I do remember that the ultimate torture for them was to have their hair cut short. Today, those hacked up dos would be right in style. I'm not sure when women started cutting their hair short but it was probably one of the worst developments in human history. Since they looked like men they thought they should be treated like men and the Women's Equality Movement followed shortly after. And what were the men to do but give in? After all they had never encountered short haired, bra burning liberal women before. These women were nothing like their mothers.

The world has changed a lot since those early days of my youth. Now it seems that men are more vain than women. Women whack their hair short so they don't have to fool with it and men are taking Rogaine so they can have more hair to fool with. Men also spend time cultivating hair on their faces. There are mustaches, van dykes, goatees and bippys every where you look. Bippys are a new one for me they are that little piece of hair left growing below the lower lip while the rest of the face is clean-shaven. I guess their purpose is to catch any food that may dribble from your mouth and keep your chin clean.

The future can only bring more changes to our world. Men will no longer cut their hair but keep it up in a French bun and women will visit the barber once a week to get a trim. I just hope they never start putting foo foo juice on their necks. I would hate to think that they had been hanging out at one of those French Bordellos.

Yo-Yos

I hope Santa didn't bring your children new video games for Christmas this year. From what I see on the street, there is a new phenomenon sweeping the country and video games are now for the uncoordinated geeks. What am I talking about? Let me give you some hints. Sleeper, Rock the Baby, Walk the Dog, Climb the Elevator. Still don't know, maybe this will help.

Down it goes and round and round, then up it comes once more,
A yo-yo isn't happy 'til it's flung down toward the floor.
This time it almost touches but a quick jerk of the hand
Brings it back to safety, ready to go again.

It must be grasped just so and rolled from the finger thus.
One must enter a state of YO and eliminate all fuss.
It's just two tiny disks of wood with an axle and a string.
But to watch a child make a yo-yo, YO is quite an amazing thing.

That's right, folks, kids are learning that yo-yos are fun and they can do impressive tricks with them. My nephews and niece all have yo-yos and are constantly showing each other what they can make theirs do. They are actually playing together; can you imagine kids interacting with their peers in a good way? I noticed that Andy even had a little yo-yo holster on his belt so he can carry his with him wherever he goes and no one will think he has a can of snuff in his pocket.

We had yo-yos when we were young, we even did tricks with them, but don't mess with this new generation; they're too good. Jerry was probably the best with a yo-yo, but Bob Mauney was hard to beat with a spinning top. He could make those things dance. I usually ended up throwing my top too hard, it would flop over on its side and shoot under the couch, I never did get the hang of it.

Girls had toys too, they had jacks, a soft rubber ball was bounced and while it was in the air, they gathered as many jacks as they could. Jacks looked like something a Ninja might carry in his bag of tricks to throw under the tires of a runaway truck. I never got the hang of that game either.

Marbles were more to my liking. I still have a sock full of the things. We played Chase, Pig's Eye and of course Keepers. Keepers was the one that always got us in trouble at school, the teachers claimed it was a form of gambling. If you weren't very good at it, you could lose all your marbles but if you had a good steel and knew how to make it stick, you could go home with all your pockets full. Mr. Lindsay played with us sometimes but you had to watch him, he was sneaky.

We made a lot of toys from things that were readily available. A piece of string and a large button could be made into something that went whiz when the string was pulled. I don't remember what it was called but it was fun to catch a girl's hair in the string. We made whistles from a piece of bamboo, slingshots from a stick of hickory and an old inner tube and gee-haw whimmy diddles that had to be rubbed just right.

We played other games too, hide and seek; tag; freeze tag, a variation of tag during which the tagged had to stay in the same position until someone on his team tagged him again to set him free; crack the whip; red rover; stop light; Mama may I and that ever popular What's your occupation? I don't think I ever knew the rules or the purpose of What's your occupation, all I remember is that it was a form of charades and you said bum, bum, bum a lot. Crack the whip was a game for cold mornings, best played with a light snow falling and the ground slick. Five, ten, fifteen or more kids holding hands and running around at great speed, the leader trying his darndest to crack the whip and throw the last one into the bushes.

Do not be surprised if that new Playstation or Nintendo 64 sits dormant this spring or if your kids start carrying an old bulging sock to school. They have just learned that action games are better than games that play by themselves. Who knows, maybe checkers will make a comeback; Morgan Alexander did get a checkerboard for Christmas. Can Hula-Hoops be far behind?

With the Y2K bug looming on the horizon, could these kids be preparing for the impending crash of all video and computer games? Maybe the rest of us should try to remember how to do things the old ways, too.

Lost Ghosts

I was recently caught by the traffic light at the Bethel Gin. Yeah, that's right, there is a traffic light at the Bethel Gin intersection. In fact, Lake Wylie now has more traffic lights than the big city of Clover. While stopped, I chanced to look around at all the changes that have taken place over the last ten years and wondered what changes the next ten years might bring.

There to my right is the new Food Lion the walls are just going up. Across the way is the new Winn-Dixie, there are already signs on the front of their building. To my left is Bethel Lumber which used to be H&S Lumber, which before that was Jim and Shelby's Mom and Pop Grocery, which long before that was the Bethel Gin. Across from the Winn-Dixie is a vacant lot that used to be the Sportsmen, which long before that was Lewis Chamber's country store. I can't even locate the site of Moss's Beer Joint, the intersection had changed so much.

I thought to myself, the ghosts that roam this area must really be confused. Moss's always had a game of Setback going on, I never understood the rules, but the games must have lasted for several years because every time I went in there, the same old men were sitting in the same booth, holding the same cards, and drinking the same beer. Out back was a pile of beer cans below the grease rack. Jimmy Buffett may have said it best, "Imagine all the heartaches and tears in twenty-seven years of beers". Big Boy Cloninger used to hang out there. All the kids would laugh at him because he never drove his old pickup over thirty miles per hour. I stopped laughing after Jerry and I helped him and Ace load hay one year. He drove thirty through the fields too. Thirty is fast when you're trying to hit a pickup with a bale of hay.

The Bethel Gin is where Daddy took corn to be ground. I'm not sure why you had to grind corn, it had something to do with the fermentation process. Big Guy Davis was in charge of the ginning operation. I remember the place was always dusty and smelled kind of sweet. It was a great place for a kid. We would back the truck up to a chute and shovel the corn into this great gaping mouth with iron teeth that spun around and stripped the kernels from the cobs. From there the kernels would go into the vast inner workings and eventually come out of this huge silo looking thing that reached all the way to the ceiling. They were fifteen or twenty feet across and the bottoms were cone shaped with a little spout where you held a feed sack to collect whatever you were having ground. We used those feed sacks for shirt material.

Right about the middle of the new Winn-Dixie probably in the Deli section is where Mr. Charlie Neal lived. Of course, back then, it was a hilltop, so I guess if Mr. Charlie's ghost is roaming around, looking for home, he will be up in the rafters, somewhere. When I was a kid, he cut my hair. I'm not sure why we trusted him, he didn't have a hair on his head.

Chamber's store was where we all hung out. I guess because Marion had a car although he couldn't drive worth a dam. One winter, we cut donuts in Jim and Shelby's parking lot and Marion lost it headlong into the ditch. Of course to hear him tell it, it was just to see how scared the rest of us could get.

So, what will the next ten years bring? The Food Lion and the Winn-Dixie will each be vying for our grocery dollars. The Home Depot will supply all of our DIY needs. Kmart will move in and become our one stop shopping center. Then there will be an Office Max, because we will all be working from home. There will be restaurants of every description, Mill Creek Mall will be the hangout for the teenage set, except for the new River Rat that now sits atop the Mall and rotates once every thirty minutes to allow each diner a view of the river. Crowder's Creek will sport the Mugsy and Dell Bar and Grill, a sports bar for the true Hornet's fan. The Holiday Inn will face the new high rise Buster Boyd Bridge on Lake Wylie and have nightly entertainment for your dining pleasure. Unless you know where these places are, they will be difficult to find because of the new overlay rules, which won't allow any signs whatsoever.

The car behind me is blowing his horn, because the light has turned green. One of those impatient Gastonia people who think the speed limit through here is sixty-five, I guess. Everyone is in such a hurry these days. I look again to the right and catch a glimpse of a few old men sitting at a table, drinking Carling Black Label, right in the middle of the intersection. One of them yells Setback and raps his knuckles on the table. The Gastonite passes and gives me a dirty look, I nod politely When I look back for the card game, the old men are gone, but then again, so are a lot of other things.

Mike A. Marr, Sr.

Polk Salad and Creasy Greens

I was looking at some grocery receipts the other day and was shocked. It suddenly dawned on me that everyone was worrying about the wrong things. The price of the groceries wasn't the problem although that did seem unreasonable it was the date. Yes, that's right the date printed on the bottom of the receipt was 4/6/99.

Why hasn't the news media picked up on this potentially dangerous situation? We hear all about banks going under and airplanes falling from the sky, but no one has mentioned the fact the grocery stores are not ready for Y2K. I can see it all now New Years Day, 2000 the Winn-Dixies and the Food Lions throughout Lake Wylie will completely disappear. When their computers revert to 1900, they will realize that the stores don't even exist yet. First the lights will dim and then go out. The freezers will stop and all the prepackaged meats will turn back into cows, sheep and pigs. Pheasant and chickens will run rampant down the aisles. All the vegetables will shrivel up and turn into seeds to feed the wild animals.

I don't know about you but I'm concerned. I'm not so sure that I want to learn how to farm again. I grew up that way and if I remember correctly it was a hard life. We had to hoe beans every day, summer and winter, 365 days a year. I don't know why but we did. I almost lost a toe hoeing beans. I was barefooted and caught the end of my big toe with the hoe, pulled the nail right off. Daddy took me to the house, bandaged it and brought me right back to the row where I had left off. That was the last time I tried that tactic. Then you had to pick beans, bushels and bushels of beans. We sold some but we ate most of them. Now that I think about it, those were the best green beans I ever ate.

You had to pull corn, for those of you from up North that means removing the ears from the stalks. My Grandma said you should never tell secrets in the cornfield because you never knew when the ears were listening. We pulled corn for rosineres (roasting ears). We pulled corn to fill the corncrib so the animals would have food through the winter. After all the corn was pulled, we pulled fodder and then shocked the stalks. This was so you would have something nice to put the pumpkins around at Halloween. Yes we raised pumpkins, too.

I remember one year when my mother was working second shift in the mill and Daddy and I had to fend for ourselves. You never knew what you might have for supper he would cook anything. Once he sent me to the pumpkin patch to pull blooms. I didn't ask any questions I knew better. By the way fried, pumpkin blooms taste like fish. I guess I should check with Helen Crawford to see if there was any nutritional value in them.

Wild onions were another staple at our house, we didn't grow them especially, but we did use what God gave us. They make a great base for homemade vegetable soup if you could get by the smell. Another house specialty was polk salad. Polk grows wild all over Lake Wylie and in the hands of the proper chef makes a delicious greens dish. Speaking of greens, you could always find wild creasy greens to make a sandwich. Just wash them off and slap them on a piece of light bread with a smear of mayonnaise. Talk about good eating.

We weren't exactly rich but you couldn't tell it from our table. There was always meat of some kind. We raised our own beef, pork and chickens and slaughtering day was a sight to behold. People from all around came to help out and were always paid with a good cut of meat. The one meal I miss the most was a piece of tender loin from a fresh kill with freshly churned butter and a big slice of cornbread.

Shortly after Diane and I were married we ate dinner with Pop. When she asked what the meat might be he told her it was deer. It was only after she had eaten her second helping that he finished his description, dear old billy goat. She asked for thirds.

So, if old Y2K knocks out the grocery stores we will survive and you know what, it just might be fun. I think I'll teach Farley and Spenser to pull a plow and start planting a couple of acres of beans tomorrow. Anyone want to learn to hoe, it's good exercise.

Mike A. Marr, Sr.

Dear Old Bethel School

In 1957 I was finally old enough to go to Dear Old Bethel School. Being born in December has disadvantages other than Christmas; you end up waiting a year to go to school. I was ready at five years because my sister-in-law had spent many hours drilling me in the 3R's and so when I got there, the learning was too easy. I spent a lot of time daydreaming and looking out the window. I remember getting up and sitting in someone else's desk during arithmetic. Today, I would be diagnosed with Attention Deficit Disorder and would spend the rest of my life taking some kind of chemical.

Miss Alma McClure, my first grade teacher, had a cure for ADD. With her hands on her hips and a ruler in one, she could stare you into paying attention.

Dear Old Bethel (dear and old are not adjectives, that was what everyone called the place) was a huge brick structure with twelve foot ceilings and nine-foot windows. The cafeteria was an add-on block building behind the school and had the best food on earth, thanks to Mrs. Currence, except the hominy. You could also get Eskimo Pies after lunch if you had the money.

Danny Brandon and I were roughing it up under the canopy that joined the lunchroom and school one-day when I got pushed into Vonda Horne and made her drop her Eskimo Pie. She kicked me right in the belly and doubled me over gasping for air. Jim Jackson helped me into the building and we immediately got stopped by Mrs. Riddle, the third grade teacher, who wanted to know what had happened. Not being a Snitch and also not being able to breathe I kept quiet.

Jim said " Vonda kicked him in the belly."

Mrs. Riddle always the teacher corrected Jim "You mean stomach, don't you, Jim?"

That didn't make my belly feel much better but I was glad that I had learned something new, and would not go to Mrs. Riddle the next time someone kicked me in the belly. That woman had no compassion. I have since forgiven Vonda, but I may never get over Mrs. Riddle's attitude.

Hero of Bullfrog Hill

During recess, we played games that would probably seem foreign to today's children. We would crack the whip, where everyone held hands as the leader ran around the school yard making quick turns and backtracking to try to get the last kid airborne. We played Red Rover, another handholding game where two teams held hands at opposite ends of a field and called out for one of the more popular kids to try to break through their barrier. If you failed you joined that team, if you succeeded you brought one of theirs back with you. We also played something the girls thought up called "What's Your Occupation?" a charade game in which you acted out your future career in front of the other team. If they guessed correctly, everyone ran to base. Those that got caught were kissed or something.

Mrs. Barnett's second grade class was on the short hall that led to the lunchroom with the classroom door facing the outside door. We were the first ones out at recess and watched the big kids jump out the window in the main hall, if no teacher was watching. It was a good seven-foot drop to the ground and we were too small to try it. Besides, Mr. Lindsay's sixth grade room was just across the hall from that window and if he caught you, he would eat you. Many elementary children were never heard from after jumping out that window.

There is a good deal of concern today about lead based paint on playground equipment and children eating it. We had a merry-go-round, a jungle gym, a giant slide, a swing set and seesaws but I don't remember any of them ever having paint on them. If they had, I'm sure we would have had more sense than to eat it. This sounds more like a parenting problem than a playground problem. Maybe they have a vitamin deficiency.

That old merry-go-round was faster than a '55 Chevy. With two husky sixth graders inside it, pushing for all their worth you could hold on to the bars and fly parallel to the ground. At least until your fingers gave out and you went shooting off towards the jungle gym. We knew how to have a good time. The swings were about twelve feet high with heavy chains and solid wood seats. You could get those things going fast enough and high enough that the chains would go slack at the top and you were weightless for an instant. That was when you were expected to bail out. We were preparing for the Space Program and didn't even know it.

On rainy days, we all gathered in the auditorium during recess, to watch films. There were "The Three Stooges" and my favorite "Abbott and Costello". I never figured out how Lou drank water form that tin can when he was underwater. Today's children don't get enough "Abbott and Costello". They could learn a lot from those two. There were also days when we had to watch documentaries like "The Products of Brazil" or "The Average Rainfall in the Amazon". I kept hoping Tarzan would show up in that one, but he never did.

Baseball was the big thing at Dear Old Bethel and it was every boy's goal to be able to play on the big field. Mr. Lindsay ran the show and would always play with us. He would cheat, however. One day Glenn Jackson was pitching and Mr. Lindsay hit a linedrive right back at him catching him in the shin and taking him down. Mr. Lindsay ran straight to the pitcher's mound to check on Glenn. In the meantime, our team grabbed the ball and threw him out at first. Would you believe he made us play it over and got to bat again? It wasn't our fault he ran the wrong way.

In Mrs. Fran Jackson's fourth grade class, I learned about the "War Between the States" and haven't been able to call it the "Civil War" since.

"There was nothing civil about it" she used to say, "There were two separate countries at war with each other. Civil implies internal and the South was not a part of the North." I still get distressed when TV shows like "The Civil War" are aired. I can't help thinking that they have to be a Yankee plot of some kind and will distort the truth. History is so malleable anyway.

Mrs. Jackson had a roving eye and at lunch she could look at her plate with one eye and watch the entire class with the other. Don't get me wrong, I loved that old woman dearly. She is solely responsible for my education and my yearning for knowledge. She could not stand incompetence and to this day, I have a problem with it myself. I remember her throwing a history book the entire length of the classroom once, because a girl asked her the same question for the third time. I also saw her grab William Sexton by the shoulders and shake him like a dishrag because he couldn't understand the math lesson. She literally shook some sense into him.

Hero of Bullfrog Hill

Miss Ruth Baird taught fifth grade and was the easiest of the teachers at Dear Old Bethel. Easy in that she didn't throw things or yell at the students. She did give a lot of homework though. During one six-week period, we had to do a health project that covered six chapters in our book supposedly a short essay on each chapter. We were to turn them in on Friday. Being lazy by nature and procrastinative by choice, remember I should have been ADD, I didn't have mine and begged Miss Baird for the weekend to finish it. After working day and night all weekend, I turned in six posters with drawings depicting the gist of each chapter. I got an "A" and she never knew that I hadn't even read those chapters.

Dear Old Bethel burned down in a lightning storm in the summer of 1959 and was replaced with a modern brick and glass structure. Bethel School never really replaced Dear Old Bethel and nothing was the same after that. The auditorium and lunchroom are now a cafeterium where you use the same chairs for eating and programs. All the old teachers are gone from Bethel in one way or another and we'll miss each one. The old lunchroom is still there but is now used for storage and the Eskimo Pies aren't as good as they used to be. I think I'll go to the store and buy one now, bet you, it will cost more than a dime.

Baseball Moms

Don't you hate it when your friends start bragging on their children? The only thing worse is when they present proof to back up their claims. A good friend of mine recently showed me a copy of a Little League score book sheet with eighteen strikeouts. In Little League, there are only six innings, so you do the math. Scott didn't pitch a no-hitter but he still had quite an accomplishment.

Diane and I have two nephews playing Little League and we try to make it to at least one of their games every season. I had the brilliant idea of killing two birds with one stone; we would attend the game in which they played each other. Major mistake. It was extremely tough to pull for Craig's pitching while Jesse was at bat, especially with the bases loaded, two outs, and a full count, I couldn't watch. Anyone who knows Diane knows that she is the World's greatest cheerleader. It was almost painful to watch her sitting there swallowing her OOH, OOH OOHs. Once, she jumped up with fist skyward and almost yelled, but caught herself and bit down hard on her tongue, instead and gave me one of those looks like "This is all your fault". We will go to our nephew's games again, but not if they are playing each other.

Organized baseball for children was invented for their parents, not the kids. Its purpose is to humiliate the players while making morons out of their parents. If the kids really wanted to play ball, they would choose up sides, find a cow pasture and enjoy themselves. The following day, the teams would be completely different (just like the Pros) as new team leaders got to choose up sides. They would learn much more about sportsmanship, their own limitations and life in general than they ever will in a game designed for the entertainment of the fans.

Don't misunderstand, I'm not opposed to organized baseball, anything is better than allowing these kids to sit in the house and play video baseball. The truth is, I actually coached for a while. There are still a few people in the neighborhood to whom I owe apologies. I was not very tolerant of incompetent umpires. Coaching children brought out a side of me that I didn't like very much, and I am sure many of today's parents will reflect on their game-day statements and wonder how they ever sank to that level.

Hero of Bullfrog Hill

Children should not be exposed to the examples parents set at a Little League game.

At the above mentioned game, I watched one parent running around ranting and raving about this call or that call and couldn't help asking him, "You never did get to put somebody's eye out, did you?" He looked at me like I was crazy and I told him. "Your Mother always said you wouldn't be happy till you put somebody's eye out." He was thoughtful for a moment and then went back to yelling. I don't suppose you should get philosophical at a Little League game, but I have always felt that certain things should be pointed out.

For pure entertainment, you should take in one of the many T-Ball games played at "Dear Old Bethel". These kids are between five and seven years old and have a ball. There are ten batters per inning, no outs and no score keeping. The ball is hit from a huge golf tee and if it reaches the outfield, chaos ensues. While the batter is running the bases, all the outfielders and at least three infielders are rolling in the grass, fighting for the ball. The coach yells "Throw it to the pitcher". Of course the pitcher is watching the runner merrily skipping from second to third and the ball gets away again and another wrestling match starts up. From the sidelines, you hear things like:

"Tyler, get your glove out of your mouth" or,

"NO, stay in there, you can go to the bathroom after the game" or,

"Don't wear your hat backwards, you look silly".

These little kids will move up eventually into a much more regulated type of baseball with outs and runs that count and unfortunate yells from the fans when they make a mistake. The one thing I'm afraid they will leave behind is the fun.

However, baseball is our National Pastime, yelling at umpires is a God-given right and all of these kids have a chance to make the big money in the Pros, if we can just get the coach to play them enough to show their stuff.

Mike A. Marr, Sr.

Whole Language Spelling Bee

Did you hear about the Whole Language Spelling Bee? It is going into its sixth week and no one has missed a word yet.

What is going on in the school systems these days? The teachers aren't allowed to correct children because it may scar them for life, therefore anything they turn in has to be right, regardless of spelling, grammar or style. The problem, as I see it, is these children will someday be forced to operate in the real world, where deductions are made for lack of education.

Coming home from Long Beach this past Memorial Day, I noticed a sign proclaiming free "financeing". Now, I don't know about you, but I would worry about financing a contract with someone who can't even spell the word. The fine print would have to be thoroughly checked out.

A term that is catching on in the business world is "Grow your Business". I was contacted by a headhunter recently who kept my attention up to the point where she informed me that her client liked to buy small businesses and "Grow" them. Her client may help my business grow, but it will grow on its own. The lady with the bad accent who is remodeling her cottage with the help of the Yellow Pages uses this term in her advertising. She says, "The Bell South Yellow Pages will help you grow your business." AARRGH! I'm sorry, that just really irks me.

I remember spelling bees at "Dear Old Bethel". If you missed a word, you sat down, a simple concept. At the end, only one person was left standing and that person received the respect that he or she was due. Of course there were those who called the winner names, but inside they truly wanted to be that person and probably studied a little to try to win next time. In the third grade I missed the word, Arctic, I had never been there, didn't even know where it was and certainly didn't intend to go there. How was I to know that there was a "C" in the middle of it. Mrs. Riddle pointed out to me that not only was there a "C" in the middle of Arctic, but it was called the Arctic Sea. I have never misspelled that word again.

Another word that gave me headaches was separate, then I learned that there was "a rat" in separate. It stuck with me.

Hero of Bullfrog Hill

There are many rules in spelling that stay with us the rest of our lives. Hidden away in the clutter of our minds, just waiting for a chance to come out are the ie and ei rules. "I" before "e" except after "C" or pronounced as "a" as in neighbor or weigh. The rule for dropping the "e" and adding "ing" still shows its ugly little head now and then as in the sign mentioned above.

"Its" is another troublesome word even though it's so small. The apostrophe is only used when a contraction of "it is" is intended.

I realize that most people could care less about how other people spell, but I'm somewhat anal-retentive. I have been told that I would argue with a signpost and why not, if that signpost is wrong. Traveling down highway 5 toward Blacksburg, there is a sign that says "Blacksburg 1 Mile", not two hundred feet further is a sign proclaiming "Blacksburg City limit". That's not right and, yes, I do argue with it every time I go by there.

There are admittedly exceptions to every rule. My brother, Dewitt doesn't like the use of phonics. One argument is the word, ghoti. We have all eaten ghoti and several of us like to ghoti on the weekends. If you break this word down, the "gh" is from laugh, the "o" is from women and the "ti" is from motion, fish.

Right now, I don't really need any <u>financeing</u>, my business is <u>growing</u> on <u>its</u> own and I think I'll drive the <u>extra mile</u> to Blacksburg and go <u>ghoting.</u>

Mike A. Marr, Sr.

Space Heroes

You hear a great deal, these days, about kids with ADD or Attention Deficit Disorder. When we were at Dear Old Bethel, there was no such thing. There were kids who were slow learners, kids who didn't read very well and kids who just didn't care, but there was no ADD, no LD and no dyslexia. Today, no one wants to take responsibility and so the powers that be come up with all kinds of excuses to explain little Johnny's problem.

As for Attention Deficit disorder, I think it is a learned trait. Children learn it from their parents. How many of you can name the little robotic investigator roaming around on the Martian landscape? I admit that I had to look it up and if you don't know, then you will have to look it up, too. How many of you can name the very first manmade object launched into space? Probably several more than have kept up with the Martian expedition.

In October 1957, Russia sent *Sputnik* into orbit around the Earth and the whole world was amazed. This was during the Cold War and the fear of attack from Outer Space had everyone frightened. The following January, we Americans sent *Explorer* on its way from Cape Canaveral and the "Space Race" was on. In i961, Yuri Gagarin became the first human to orbit the Earth in a capsule named Vostic II. On May 5th of that year, Alan Shepard, Jr. became the first American to go into space. His flight and the following flight by Gus Grissom were sub-orbital. It wasn't until February 1962, that John Glenn completed three orbits around the Earth and was truly known as the first Astronaut. Gordon Cooper's 22 orbit flight in May, 1963 ended the *Mercury project* and shortly thereafter the *Gemini* and the *Apollo* projects led to Neil Armstrong's walk on the Moon on July 20,1969.

What does any of this have to do with ADD? How many of the above names and dates do you remember? How many of you remember sitting in class and watching Alan Shepard's complete flight from liftoff to splashdown? At times there was nothing to see but the men in Mission Control watching their monitors and waiting. We waited with them with our eyes glued to the television monitor. We really didn't know what we were looking for, but we realized that history was being made and somehow we were a part

Hero of Bullfrog Hill

of it. After the little capsule crashed into the Ocean, we sat perfectly still and listened to the announcers as they described everything from the rolling waves to the rotation of the helicopter blades. As the capsule's hatch was blown away, we saw why we had been waiting patiently. A True Hero emerged from that now foreign vessel and the whole class cheered and yelled as one. There were even a few tears falling here and there. Was there a deficit of attention, I don't think so. We all realized that something Big had just been witnessed and we were there. We knew that someday, maybe in our lifetime, man would walk on the moon, visit the other planets and even live in Space. As we looked around the room, we wondered which one of us would be the first Human to set foot on Martian soil.

Times have changed, people have changed, technology is running rampant and our brains are bombarded constantly with new information. Maybe it is time to rethink our excuses. Maybe we should look closer at our teaching methods. Maybe today's kids have evolved into new humans who totally lack the ability to sit down and watch a two hour space flight without understanding how it could have been done easier and better. Maybe ADD is a warning and a message that the future will be fast paced and there will be no room for the old slow ways we have become accustomed to accepting without question.

I'm trying to keep up with the new information arriving daily from the Martian rover, but find that it is tedious and boring. I wonder if the first manned Martian flight will even make the six o'clock News or if we will be too interested in what's happening on *True Stories of the Highway Patrol* to even care.

Mike A. Marr, Sr.

Board of Education

School has started, please watch for children. There have been a lot of changes in the Clover School District since I was a student. Griggs Road Elementary is up and running and I understand that two new schools are scheduled to specifically handle the Lake Wylie overload. With home building starting soon in The Landing, I suppose that it is only natural for the new schools to be built close by. However, it just doesn't seem right for children to do anything but go to Dear Old Bethel and then Dear Old Clover. If you're not a Blue Eagle then what are you?

I watched the idea of school spirit change with my own sons and I guess it is inevitable that it will change even more with the next generation. My generation wouldn't think of missing a Blue Eagle home football game while Arnie and Robb only go occasionally. They both played for the team but they didn't develop the attachment of past graduates and with the new High School, I'm not sure where their allegiances will lie. I suppose that there will be a cross district rivalry but it will never match the rivalries we had with the York Green Dragons or the Fort Mill Yellow Jackets. People would practically lay down their lives for the honor of their schools.

I really feel sorry for the teachers today. With no corporal punishment, they are at the mercy of the students, another example of what is so wrong with this country. As in so many businesses that have to deal with unions, the inmates are in charge of the asylum.

We had teachers who were in absolute control. No one would have ever thought of talking back to Mrs. Bodie or even poor old Miss Sills. Miss Sills taught algebra but now that I look back at it, I'm not sure she understood anything about the subject. She would say, "I wish I had a nickel for every time I have explained this." Hoyle Beachum stood up one day and answered, "Miss Sills, I'll loan you a nickel." I don't think she understood his comment either.

I loved Mrs. Bodie, not because of her beauty which I'm sure was inner, but because she taught me to understand and appreciate literature. She could make you hear those coins squeal as *Silas*

Marner squeezed them. You could also feel the total disappointment in the voice of *Julius Caesar* as he whispered, "Et tu, Brute".

There were also teachers whose job was to be the enforcer of the law. Most of these teachers were coaches but one that I remember well was Mr. Tom Adams guidance counselor. With football practice right after school, players knew better than to get into trouble and have to go to detention hall. The coaches would come after you give you your licks and that was that. I had just nailed my new horseshoe taps on my Weejuns and Joe Baird and others were trying to see how fast they could push me down the band hall when Mr. Tom stepped out of his office. We zipped past him at thirty miles per hour and the detention slips came just as quickly. Coach Fitzpatrick found out and got us all out of incarceration but there was Hell to pay.

Coach Jerry Frye gave me my first licks in High School. I leaned over the water fountain and with one blow he lifted my feet off the floor. I remember the paddle had little holes drilled through it and the words "Board of Education" engraved on it. That man could eliminate some of the drug problems schools have today. Few of the Lady Teachers gave licks but they all knew where to send you when the time came.

I really don't think that High School should be like a prison but some form of discipline is definitely needed. Maybe the Board of Education should look around for Coach Frye's "Board of Education" and apply it in the proper fashion That being much like a tennis forehand, form a "C with the backswing and make solid contact on the follow through.

Since we have two new schools maybe we could start them off on the right track. Let's put control back in the hands of the teachers and hire a few enforcers to make sure it stays there. I'm sure that Jerry Frye has retired but Mr. Charlie Brown is bound to know someone who could do just as well.

Mike A. Marr, Sr.

Reunions

Today, we are going to the King family reunion. The Ford family reunion is later this month followed by the Robinson and Marr reunions. Sometimes, I wonder how families get so far apart that they need to reunite each year. We will see people at these reunions that we haven't seen in years even though some of them live within spitting distance. One common thread through all these get togethers is everyone is getting older.

On a recent trip to the beach I stopped in a local CVS to pick up some suntan lotion, a bottle of Coke and some sinus tablets. I walked up to the checkout where the young lady asked for some ID. I looked at the three items and wondered which one was no longer sold to minors. As I reached for my wallet I asked "Why?"

She said, "It's senior citizen day."

Highly offended I backed up from the counter and asked, "Does this look like the body of a senior citizen?"

Two weeks later, I went by McDonald's for a cup o coffee. The young girl at the counter said, "That will be twenty-five cents."

I said, "That's cheap enough."

She told me that seniors got coffee at a discount and I thought to myself, "What's going on here?" Now, I can remember when the moustache was completely dark and the hair didn't look like salt and pepper but I don't feel any older. I can't run a 10.8 hundred anymore and there are some cracking joints when I get up in the morning but I never liked mornings anyway.

My children are getting old. Robb is a daddy and Arnie will soon be thirty. I can remember when thirty was over the hill. When I look back at thirty now I realize that I didn't take Bio-flex and I didn't wear a knee brace to dance. I also realized that in just a few more years Diane and I could dance in the Masters division where the couples combined age is over the century mark.

I suppose what is causing all this reflection is the thirtieth anniversary of our high school graduation or as Gail Clinton likes to call it, our third ten-year anniversary. We are having a reunion.

We graduated from Clover High School in 1969 with eighty-nine seniors, six of whom have passed on, some are single, some married and some have been married several times. Like most classes we have doctors and lawyers but I don't think we have any Indian chiefs. Some have stayed in touch and some haven't been heard of since graduation. We have a reunion every five years and the same ones keep showing up and usually it is the ones from out of town that come while the locals don't get involved.

I have talked to a few who plan to come who have never come before. I suppose that after all these years the bickering and petty differences have lessened and everyone just wants to see how everyone else is getting along. I'm sure there will be pictures of grandchildren to brag about and people will be able to laugh at their own losses and gains, hair and weight that is.

Dennis McClure is planning to come to our reunion for the first time and we may have to have a foot race. He was the only one who could outrun me and I want to see if he still can.

We will drink a little, laugh a little and maybe even cry a little. We will talk about the ones who don't come and try to figure out why they are still mad. We will talk about the ones who are no longer with us and try to figure out why.

When we get older we learn that things we thought were most important are now trivial and friendship is the most important thing there is. During our school years, it seemed the things that made us different were the most important, now maybe we will find out that we are all more alike than we could have ever imagined.

As for those senior citizen discounts, ya'll keep giving them out. I'm learning to accept them and they're not that bad.

Mike A. Marr, Sr.

Some Folks Should Not Drive

Julius Caesar was warned to "Beware the Ides of March". Today, it's the Ides of April that concerns most of us, but with the help of my trusty new friend, the Internet, I was able to get my taxes done on time and didn't have to search the world over for the right forms. The Internet is a wonderful place to spend time, but if you aren't careful, you could spend too much time there. The first thing you know it's two in the morning and you still haven't found the information you were originally seeking.

We have a few sites bookmarked, Barnes & Noble, Hampton Hamster, the Internal Revenue Service and others that are favorites for some reason but I can't remember why. E-mail is the one essential of the Internet without which, I'm not sure how we ever got along. Gale Copeland lives just far enough away to make a phone call long distance, so we get mail from her daily. Sometimes the inbox is spilling over onto my desk with jokes, cute pages and other things that she has forwarded for our enjoyment.

The most recent items from this friend included ICQ, (get it I seek you, those webmasters are pretty sharp). This little download allows us to chat over the computer. Occasionally, late at night, I will hear Diane cackling away in the office and immediately know that she and Gale are chatting.

Gale keeps asking me if I have had a random chat yet and I tell her no, with all the weirdoes out there, I haven't. That is a lie, however, I did meet another Marr from Maine. I thought at first that he was just a kid, his typing was very childish, anyway. Then I learned that was the way one corresponds on the Internet. No capitalization and no rules of grammar or punctuation are needed. You just type away faster than your correspondent does if possible.

When I first heard the term, Univac, I wanted to know all about how it worked and what it could do. I never imagined that someday I would use a computer with ten times its power on a daily basis, and what do I do with it, chat with Gale.

I lost my bus license in the eleventh grade, literally. Jimmy Burton and I were riding some wild ride at the Gaston County Fair and my billfold came out and opened, papers were flying everywhere. Jimmy would grab something from the air and ask, "Is this any good?" My response was usually "No, Let it go". My license was one of the items that got let go, which was fine because I didn't intend to drive my senior year. I didn't know at the time that Gale would end up with my route.

I was her first stop every morning and after the first few days of school, I drove the rest of the route. Gale wasn't a bad driver but she always did like to chat and I would rather she chatted form the passenger seat when I was on the bus. The arrangement worked well for both of us, she drove to my house and I finished the route. It would have been a perfect year, too, had it not been for that old biddy who turned me in.

Near the end of the morning run, we had to maneuver through the narrow streets of Clover to get to Kinard Elementary. At one particular intersection you had to make a wide right turn just to get the bus around the corner. When we got there, the aforesaid biddy was sitting in the middle of the road as if she owned it. Being a creative and innovative kind of driver and also in a bit of a hurry, I whipped past her on the wrong side, there was more room on that side anyway. The kids didn't mind they got a kick out of it, especially the look on her face.

By the time we reached the High School, old biddy had called and reported our bus number and of course, Gale got called to the office. I don't remember whether she turned me in or took the blame. Maybe, I will e-mail tonight and ask. Aren't computers wonderful?

Mike A. Marr, Sr.

Tough Teachers

As you all know, I have been unmerciful to our poor friends who have moved here to escape the bitter cold of the northern states. There is one young lady, however, to whom we all owe an apology. I'm speaking of the teacher in Charlotte who used masking tape to control an unruly child. God Bless her. The poor girl moved here from New York and was placed in a class full of children whose speech surely irritated her senses with their long drawn out vowel sounds and then to have one who would not be quiet at all had to grind her last nerve. My only regret is that she didn't use super glue.

Southern teachers today would never resort to such a method of punishment. We are too polite to do something like that, but I would be willing to bet that there isn't a teacher in York County who hasn't thought about it, especially those at Grigg's Road Elementary who happened to get stuck with my nephew Andy. He can talk a blue streak and has not quite grasped the concept of authority.

After seeing the young victim's mother on the nightly news, I'm pretty sure she has never been disciplined either. I can just hear her now, "You can't tell me what to do. I'll tell my mom." Well, mom, things are changing and the adults are going to have to take over.

Dr. Spock is responsible for all the troubles the schools are in these days. Telling us that we shouldn't spank our children because they may become traumatized has created a class of kids that are traumatizing the rest of the world. The laws of physics tell us that for every action there is an equal and opposite reaction. To my way of thinking masking tape is a good reaction.

When we were in school, we had authority figures. W.B. Lindsay, better known as Wooly Booger (I can say that now that I'm grown) was the principal and being sent to his office meant a paddling was forthcoming. He usually paddled first and then asked questions later. If things got out of hand, they called in the big gun, T.G. Kinard the superintendent. He was better known as Two Gun and a hush fell over the entire school when his car pulled into the parking lot, someone was going to die.

Discipline started in the first grade with Miss Alma McClure. I don't remember her ever striking anyone but she had "The Stare". That woman could look at you so hard your mom felt it and would ask about it when you got home. Miss Alma missed a day now and then and this was not a good thing. Her substitute was a wiry little old thing who kept a ruler in her hand at all times. She thought the main purpose of that ruler was to crack knuckles and used it on numerous occasions. Some of mine are still crooked. I can't remember her name but I'm sure there are several who remember that little ruler.

Mrs. Maude Barnett held court in the second grade and was the sweetest lady you have ever met. Right!! Third grade was Mrs. Helen Riddle and her forte was tongue-lashing. She could tell you things that made your skin crawl; most had to do with your upbringing and how miserably your poor parents had failed. Mrs. Fran Jackson, a true Confederate Grandam took care of the fourth graders. She was a woman of few words and could pick you up by the shoulders and shake you like a dishrag. She also had the evil eye. I have seen her eat lunch with one eye on her plate and the other scanning the table for troublemakers. Hopefully, lunch included onions, which meant Mrs. Fran would sleep until the busses came at 3:00. Miss Ruth Baird taught fifth grade and really was a sweetheart. You could get away with anything in her class. We once had to do an essay per Chapter in Health, which were all due at the end of the semester. Being lazy and not very good at writing, I suggested that I was doing a special project with a poster for each chapter. She bought it and I spent the entire weekend drawing.

None of these people would make it in today's school system. Back talk would lead immediately to a backhand and they would all have used duct tape on a mouthy student, not only taping her mouth but also taping her to her chair. A gun at school would have ended up in Mrs. Barnett's science room with each student having the opportunity to fire it.

Again, let me say that to the Yankee teacher with the masking tape, my hat is off. If we only had more like her we might avoid some of the incidents that are happening in our schools. If we are not going to discipline our children at home, let's at least give the

Mike A. Marr, Sr.

teachers authority to use what ever methods they deem necessary to maintain an educational atmosphere.

Can't You Read the Signs?

The sign says you've got to have a membership card to get inside. Do this, don't do that, can't you read the sign? I read somewhere that the average parents spends about thirty-seven seconds a day in conversation with their children. That is less time than it takes to watch a commercial on television. Is it any wonder that our kids are blowing each other away at school? The poor things just don't know any better. No one has told them about right and wrong so they pick up their morals from some strange sources.

My dad would spend more time than that telling me why he was beating the crap out of me. Believe me, he never had to repeat any of those lessons. Someone said it all started when they removed prayer from the public schools. If corporal punishment were reinstated in the school system prayer would not be far behind. Some of my most fervent supplications were following a misdemeanor at Junior High. The threat of spanking instills a sense of awe in children that can be translated as respect for the teachers. With this comes an understanding of respect for other people. As much as we want to teach our kids that all men are created equal, it is still necessary for someone to be in charge. At home that is the parent's job.

Daddy was not well educated but he knew things before they happened. He could read the signs. He tried his best to pass this ability along to me and spent hours explaining why some days were good for planting and some days were good for fishing. He would plow through the Farmer's Almanac and plan his spring planting. "You plant corn when the signs are in the feet"; he would tell me, "And you harvest when they are in the bowels." I later learned that the signs he was talking about were the same ones that are used in bars as in "Hey babe, what's your sign?" It never dawned on me that what he was telling me could someday be useful.

He also knew when to fish and where to fish. We would go down to Crowder's Creek and he would say, "Cast over there under that willow right at the edge of the shadow". Without question I followed his lead and always got a bite almost immediately. He knew fishing signs but I wasn't smart enough to learn them. I remember his last few years, sitting in front of the window his left side partially paralyzed watching the world go by. I wish now that I had figured out a way to take him fishing and maybe pick up on some of those signs.

He did teach me how to plant a garden, hunt game and how to raise hogs and beef. He was firmly convinced that those were the most important skills he could pass along. "The time will come when you will have to fence in your garden to keep the neighbors out", he would say. "They are going to be hungry and the one who can feed them is the one who will be in charge. Forget about the politicians and business people, farmers will be the important ones in the future."

I look at what is happening in California with the power crisis and wonder if the old man really could read the signs. A computer isn't much good if there isn't any power to make it operate.

He taught me how to handle a gun and when my kids were old enough he taught them. He said those skills might come in handy someday when someone was stealing your food supply. We saw death on the farm as a part of life. Some animals had to die so we could eat. It was a grizzly aspect of growing up in the country. I could never imagine shooting another human but he said it might come to that.

It is a real shame about these children but you have to understand where they are coming from. To them there is no future anyway. No one has taken the time to explain things to them. We are living in strange times my friends, look around you and read the sign.

What to read?

This past summer at the beach, a young boy asked Diane "What cha reading?" She replied, "Little Women by Louisa May Alcott. I haven't read it since I was a little girl." Alex said, "Why don't you just watch the movie?"

We kept Morgan one night, shortly after Pocahontas came out as a movie. She brought a copy with her and we watched it together. I mentioned to her that the real Pocahontas had gone back to England and married a gentlemen named John Rolfe. To which she quickly responded "John Smith must have changed his name."

What's wrong with kids these days? I'll tell you what's wrong with kids these days. Walt Disney is wrong. The Disney Company takes stories that we grew up with and changes them to suit their needs. Our heroes were Dumas, Scot and Tolkein. Today's heroes are Disney, Spielburg and Lucas and the overpaid actors who represent the characters that some writer created. In most instances, these movie creators not only don't write the stories they portray; they don't even acknowledge the writers.

Disney has gotten away with this habit for so long that many kids think Ol' Walt actually wrote *The Wind in the Willows* as well as *Alice in Wonderland*. When you ask them about *Alice Through the Looking Glass*, they think it is just another name for the same story. Ask a child about "Winnie the Pooh" and they know all about him. Ask that same child about A.A. Milne and their response is "Who?"

With the elections over, there is one campaign promise that really stuck in my craw. Mr. Clinton wanted to be sure that all children could read by the time they finished the third grade. I think that is a wonderful idea but what are they supposed to do the first and second year? They can't study History that requires reading. They can't do arithmetic that requires reading.

I suppose they could write, from what I understand about the Whole Language curriculum, reading is not required. You just communicate your ideas as best you can. There will be no deductions for poor spelling or poor grammar as long as you get your thought expressed. Wait, aren't children now required to attend Kindergarten. That allows them three years to develop bad habits before they are expected to learn to read.

My niece, Jann, is in the first grade and is constantly asking an adult to read this or read that to her. Wouldn't it be nice if she were able to read to the adults? When she finishes the third grade, I guess she will have that ability, if she hasn't completely lost interest. Her brother Craig is looking forward to getting a copy of the Toy Story video for Christmas this year. It is a shame that it doesn't come in written form.

When we were growing up, we learned to read before entering first grade. That way we were better able to enjoy seeing Spot run. In the summer, we looked the mailbox everyday in hopes that the "Weekly Reader" would be there. By third grade, we were completely absorbed by the adventures of Caw Caw, the Indian boy and could recite "The Midnight Ride of Paul Revere" and "The Village Smithy".

I spent many afternoons curled up in a Hobbit hole or chasing a White Rabbit or riding off with Ivanhoe or dare I say it, spending time with the Little Women. Not only did we know these works, we knew the authors, and we populated their stories with characters from our own minds. Sure, Disney came on the television every Sunday night, but we knew enough about the stories he presented to know when he made a blatant error.

Our children are growing up in a world of electronic education, where the writers are just there to fill in dialogue. It would be nice if that dialogue were grammatically correct. I have only one suggestion. This year, for Christmas, buy a child a book and if he or she is not yet in the third grade and able to read, READ it to them. Who knows, the written word could catch on.

SECTION II

SNAKES, YANKEES AND OTHER CRITTERS

Some things will just make your skin crawl while others make you feel warm all over. There is no accounting for taste. We learned to deal with snakes, polecats and the occasional bobcat but nothing prepared us for the influx of Yankees.

Mike A. Marr, Sr.

Chickens

Recently in the barber's chair, you know how men are when they are getting a haircut they have to talk, the subject of chicken came up. Cathy had eaten chicken and dumplings for lunch and I couldn't help sharing my recipe. You slow cook a whole chicken all day until it is falling off the bones and then add Pillsbury biscuits that have been stretched out of shape, season to taste. She told me that she couldn't buy whole chicken anymore because her husband got violently ill when she reached in and removed the giblets. This man is over six feet tall and weighs more than a small car, he also works as an EMT. Needless to say it surprised me that he would be squeamish about cutting up a chicken.

As a true southern gentleman, fried chicken is of course my favorite dish, however I almost overdosed on it recently. We had a family gathering and Diane fixed fried chicken, this was Sunday. Monday, Robb and Ginger came by to help wallpaper one of the bathrooms and Diane fixed fried chicken for supper. When Tuesday came around one thing led to another and before I knew it supper was late and we had fired chicken sandwiches. Wednesday was the same. Thursday I headed out of town and had lunch at Bo-Jangles, fried chicken.

I grew up on fried chicken; my mother was one of the best cooks in the world. She could put a complete meal on the table for ten people in thirty minutes and her chicken was the best you ever ate. We never had any chicken casseroles or baked chicken or chicken ala king, we had fried chicken the way God intended it to be eaten. They weren't store bought chickens either, these chickens were running through the yard earlier in the day. Momma would grab one up and throw it across the chopping block and whack his head off. Sometimes it would take twenty minutes for them stop flopping around. I bet Cathy's husband would really lose it if he had to climb in the briar patch and get one of those.

Raising chickens had another advantage, fresh eggs. Gathering eggs was one of my chores and with wild chickens it wasn't an easy task. These birds would lay anywhere. The barn loft was a minefield of nest and you had to be real careful where you stepped. They would also build nest in the woods and those were not always easy to find. Sometimes you weren't the first to locate one of these hidden nest, Old No Shoulders would beat you to it. Snakes can't resist fresh eggs. The solution was however fairly simple. A small river rock in the shape of a smooth round egg placed in the nest usually took care of it. A few days later you would find his carcass wrapped around a tree where he had been trying to crush that rock, talk about indigestion.

Snakes weren't the only varmints to steal eggs, my brother Ronnie was notorious for robbing a nest. He would take his pocketknife and tap a whole in each end and then suck all the goody right out. He had to be careful in the spring because the hens were settin'. This meant that they were planning a family and some of those eggs had the beginnings of a dibby in them.

We always marked the eggs when a hen was settin' by covering them with pencil scrawls, that way if the hen laid new eggs you could tell the difference. You could always tell when they hatched out, the yard would be full of little yellow fluffy dibs peeping at the top of their lungs.

Occasionally Mother Nature would play a trick on us and a dib would be born with two heads or maybe three legs. Daddy raised some three-legged chickens one-year, the fastest things you ever saw. A man from up north stopped by to see them. He wanted to know all about those chickens. Daddy told him that they were raised for their speed. That way they could outrun all the foxes and wild dogs.

The man said that with three legs we could make a fortune selling them to the market, as each one would have an extra drumstick. His next question was, "How do they taste?"

Daddy looked at him and said, "Dunno, we ain't never been able to catch one yet."

Spenser with an S

We recently got home from OD and it took several days to recoup. The purpose of our trip was to join in the fun at the SOS Fall Migration. SOS, for those of you from somewhere else, stands for "Society of Stranders" and Fall Migration is the gathering of shaggers from all over the United States at Ocean Drive, SC to celebrate our State Dance. If you have never been, you should take the time to go. A large time was had by all. Check around with some of your neighbors, I'm sure I saw them there.

Anyway, as I was saying, we recently got home from OD and were met at the car by a large black Lab. Diane rubbed his head and said "Spenser, did you miss us?" That's Spenser with an S like the English Poet. To which he replied "Ahhhuhhohh" which means "Yes, dear lady, I missed you badly". She then asked, "Has Robb been feeding you well?" Spenser shook his head violently from side to side slinging dog spittle everywhere. We took that as a NO, but with Spenser, you can't always tell. He looked well fed, as did Farley, the Border collie he hangs out with and so did all the cats.

Spenser doesn't talk much but with a little scratching behind the ear, he can be coaxed into telling you anything you want to hear. Farley doesn't talk at all, he just wiggles his tail to convey his emotions. What he really likes is to sit in your lap in the rocking chair, he doesn't realize that he weighs sixty to seventy pounds and there is no way he can fit on the average lap.

These are our pets, and members of our family, or possibly we are their pets and have been allowed into their pack, I've never been sure which is true.

People and pets are a strange combination, some people are dog lovers and some are cat lovers and the line is never crossed. We, however, are of the weird breed that can accept either race equally. The line of Siamese cats that have put up with us, include Satan, Lucifer, Prissy and Simon. Each was different and to some extent lived up to their names.

The most memorable dog to grace our door was a small terrier named Spotty. He came from a litter of puppies that my son, Robbie, only eight or nine at the time, watched being born. This was his first real experience with childbirth and he was fascinated.

At six weeks, Spotty moved in with us and he and Robb were inseparable. When the car took Spotty away from us, I think a part of Robb died with him. To this day, he has never cared about another animal. I guess he is the type that gives all his love to one thing, you're a lucky woman, Ginger.

In one of the Peter Seller's movies, he asked the little girl swinging on the gate, "Does your dog bite?" The little girl shakes her head and he proceeds up the walk. The dog latches on to his leg and chases him back through the gate. He looks at the girl and says, "I thought you said your dog didn't bite", to which she replies, "That, is not my dog".

Arnie is the one who always got bit. Someone would say, "Oh, that dog never bites anyone." Shortly thereafter, Arnie would come running into the house with teeth marks on his leg. Sparky had never bitten anyone. He and Arnie were roughhousing in the yard and we heard the dog give a blood-curdling yelp. When we looked out the window, we saw Arnie with Sparky's hind leg in his mouth, chewing as hard as he could. "He bit me first", Arnie cried. Sparky never did bite anyone again. Arnie still comes home with bite marks on occasion but I don't think he plays with dogs as much as he used to.

Pets are great friends and every child should have at least one. There is so much a child can learn from a pet and so many things that can be shared. You can tell a dog or a cat any secret you want without fear that someone else will find out. That is, of course, unless the dog is Spenser. Rub Spenser behind the ear and he will tell you anything you want to know.

Hog Killing Time

Boy, it was cold in November. One morning, when it got down to twenty-four degrees, I rolled the old barrel over to the fire pit, filled it with water and started the fire. Just as the water started boiling and I was finishing up with the butcher knife sharpening, I realized that I didn't have any hogs. I put the knives away, put the fire out and went back into the house and got ready for work.

Hog killing time is from the first frost until the last frost and there are a lot of rules that govern just which days are best. My dad knew all these rules and hog killing days were the busiest of the year. People came from all over to help with the dressing and everyone left with a little bit of pig at the end of the day. Everyone had a special job to do and everyone did their job without question. My sister Clare's job was to go and get the string. I asked her several years later, if she knew what the string was for and she didn't, but she knew that was her job and she always brought the best string she could find. The string was to tie the lower end of the intestine to keep the meat as clean as possible while the hog was hung from a single tree in the front yard. She didn't know it, but getting the string was a very important job for a little girl. Scraping hog hair is an art that has to be done at just exactly the right temperature. The hog is dipped into a fifty-five gallon drum of boiling water to loosen the hair. If the water is too hot, the skin comes off with the hair, too cold and the hair won't turn loose. The tried and true method of measuring the temperature is to pull your finger through the water three times. If the nail comes loose on the third pass, the water is just right.

Mama and the rest of the women were in the kitchen preparing delicacies like sausage and livermush, while the men scraped the hair form the hog. Mama yelled out the door that she wanted some backbones and ribs. JD, who still lives across the road had enjoyed a bit of Daddy's homemade corn and took Mama literally. He took the poleaxe and cut that entire hog up into backbones and ribs. Daddy yelled, "What the hell are you doing?" and JD replied, "The lady wants back bones and ribs, backbones and ribs, the Lady gets." We had no bacon that year.

Daddy was always in his glory on killing day. I think he may have had a little Vampire in him though, because he always cut the hog's throat with that huge butcher knife and then licked the blade, just to see how many people's stomachs he could turn. He also had a habit of giving some unsuspecting little kid, a ring with a pig on it. If you don't understand this ritual, ask some oldtimer.

When I was growing up, we always had an old sow and she was usually with pigs. One Summer Ronnie Bingham made a deal with Daddy to buy a boar for ten dollars. Ronnie considered himself a trader and was always making deals, although he was only ten. Ronnie kept an eye on that old sow, and when she dropped, he and I slogged through the pig lot to pick out his boar. I was half asleep and not paying any attention as Ronnie lifted one pig after another and said, "Sow, sow, sow, didn't this old gal have any males? Sow, sow." He checked each one and was satisfied they were all females. We walked back to the house and his chin was about as low as it could get.

Daddy met us smiling, "Well, did you pick out that championship boar?"

"There ain't a boar in the lot" Ronnie pouted, "I checked twice."

Daddy, knowing that there were at least three males, asked, "Just how did you go about checking them pigs, Ronnie?"

"I turned them over and everyone of them had two rows of teats. I know they were all sows." Ronnie said.

Daddy grinned, then reached out and lifted Ronnie's T-shirt, "Well looka there, I guess you must be a sow, too. After all, everyone knows there is nothing more useless than teats on a boar hog."

You have all heard the term "Anal Retentive" and how it takes years of practice to become that way. Well, we had a pig that was born anal retentive, that is, how can I put this delicately, he had a case of terminal constipation. For those of you who are afflicted with an urban upbringing, his alimentary canal had grown over and he had to be cut once a week to relieve himself. That was Dewitt's job and he didn't like it Dewitt has been a little anal retentive himself, ever since then, Believe me, no one was happier than Dewitt on that cold November morning when it was time to kill that hog. No one but maybe Clare, she didn't have to go get a string.

Mike A. Marr, Sr.

Snakes

SNAKE (sin-ache): n., a member of the reptile family; the apple salesman in the Garden of Eden, a creature of God, that he never finished, he gave it no legs; a long flexible wire for cleaning drains; a flashlight gimmick by Black and Decker. V. To cheat someone out of something, to clean out a drain; to act in a sneaky manner.

There's an old story about a man running down the road at full speed. His friend drives by and gets him to slow down enough to talk. "What's wrong with you?" his friend ask.

"I thought I saw a snake", the man replied. "But it turned out to be a stick".

"Then why are you running?", asked the friend.

"Because the stick I picked up to hit it with, turned out to be a snake."

I am so glad that cold weather has finally arrived, no more snakes. I don't dislike all snakes; dead ones are fine as long as they keep their distance.

My Daddy kept snakes in the barn to keep the rats from eating the horse feed. He also kept one in the corncrib. My fear of snakes probably started on a warm afternoon in early autumn as I was filling a bucket with corn for my cow, Claudette. Claudette was the one I sold so I could purchase a bicycle. As I leaned into the corncrib, something cold touched the back of my neck. I reached back and very accidentally grabbed the tail of a six foot long black snake. I also, very accidentally, beat it to death against the side of that shed. It was like one of those near accidents you can have in an automobile, ten minutes later. I was shaking all over.

Snakes have always been a part of growing up in Lake Wylie. My cousin Buge (short for bugle, you figure it out) and I always raced to the swimming hole in the afternoon after getting home from school. The swimming hole was in a creek that fed into Crowder's Creek behind our house. Buge, being more competitive than I, would strip his clothes off as he ran through the woods. This particular day was hot, and he was buck naked when he reached the bank over the creek. Without looking, he jumped feet first into a nest of bull snakes. I swear that he landed back on the same bank and never even got his toes wet. From that day on, we would sneak up on the swimming hole and check it out real good before jumping in.

I went night fishing with Daddy once and they weren't biting. Being young and foolish, I found an old cottonwood leaning out over the water and proceeded to climb out on it. As I shook the tree, something big fell out of the branches above me and splashed into the river. I watched that old moccasin swim away and quickly shinnied back down and grabbed my pole. I decided fishing real close to Daddy was safer than climbing trees.

Some snakes are more dangerous than others. The black snake is supposed to be a safe snake. They are what Daddy kept in the barn. They wouldn't bite you, but they could scare you to death. The Copperhead and Rattlesnake were the prominent poisonous snakes around, but they were both slow and lazy and could usually be avoided. It is said that if you have a King snake in your yard, he will keep the poisonous snakes away. When I was young, I loved to play in the woods so Daddy made sure that I could tell my snakes apart. He told me about a few, however, that to this very day, I've never laid eyes on, though I don't dare doubt their existence.

The Black Racer could come after you at over thirty miles per hour and would attack without provocation. I have never seen one, but I understand that there are still many of them in the woods around River Hills.

The Whip snake always caught his prey by the ankle and then used its tail to beat you senseless. Its tail was like a Rattlesnake, except that instead of buttons, it had sharp spikes like a war mace. I'm told they can do real damage.

Another famous snake is the Hoop snake. They prefer the rugged terrain around the edge of the lake, similar to that around Tega Cay. The Hoop snake would attack by grabbing its tail in its mouth and rolling toward its prey. At the last second, it will straighten out and drive its spike of a tail into its supper. That spike is poisonous and kills instantly. Back in the late Seventies, there were a lot of trees in Tega Cay that suspiciously died overnight. I think the Hoop snakes may have killed them.

No one has seen a Joint snake in many years. The last one I heard about was in the woods around Mill Creek. The Joint snake had a unique defense mechanism, when hit with a stick or shovel or whatever, it would break into several pieces about two inches long. Later, after its killer had left, those pieces would fit back together. It also had a long memory and would be on the lookout for anyone who had attacked it. The only way to hurt a Joint Snake is to take one of those pieces with you. That won't kill it, but it will drive it crazy trying to fit itself back together.

I know that many of you were born in the City, so the only suggestion I have for you is the same that my Daddy gave me, "If you're going to play in the woods learn your snakes."

Hero of Bullfrog Hill

Horses, Hoses and Homeless

There is an old story about the farmer who bought a cross-eyed mule. When he got it home and tried to work it, he plowed up half his crop. Not wanting to be outdone, he called the vet, who showed up the following morning

"No problem, Mr. Brown, do you have a short piece of siphoning hose?"

He sent Jake, the hired hand to the tractor shed to bring back the siphon. The vet pushed that hose up into the back end of the mule and said "Mr. Brown, step around to the front and tell me when his eyes are straight". Well, the vet blew in that hose and that old mule's eyes straightened right out.

Mr. Brown asked, "How much do I owe you?" and paid the vet forty-five dollars. He and Jake plowed all week with no problems.

The following Monday, Jake came to the house and said "Mr. Brown, them eyes is crossed up again." Mr. Brown didn't want to spend any more money so he told Jake to get the siphon hose.

He did exactly like the vet had done and Jake watched the old mule's eyes. He blew and blew and finally asked, "Jake, them eyes ain't straight yet?"

Jake shook his head and the farmer said "Well you come around here and blow awhile and let me watch."

They traded ends and Jake began removing the hose. "What are you doing? I just want you to blow in the hose," said Mr. Brown.

Jake replied, *"You* don't 'spect me to use the same end you had your mouth on, do you?" Jake had some pride.

Years ago, when I was small, my brother left for the Navy. I wasn't big enough to help around the farm and Daddy wasn't sure what he was going to do. That same summer, Barney came to the door and asked if we had any work he could do for a meal. He was dressed in oversized jeans, rolled up nearly to his knees, an old flannel shirt, and the roughest looking work shoes I had ever seen. Daddy told him to come in and eat, but he said "No sir, I would rather work first".

Barney stayed in the barn that summer and he and Daddy put in one of the biggest crops ever. Barney ate his meals with us. I remember watching him lift his fork with the same grip Mama used on a frying pan, thumb below and four fingers wrapped around the handle. After watching for a while, I realized why he ate that way, if he had used the standard method of holding his fork, he couldn't have gotten enough leverage to lift that much food.

Daddy decided that since he had Barney to help him, he was going to need another horse and mule to plow the fields. He and Barney went to see Zeb who always had something for sale and it was always the best in the country. Just ask him.

Zeb told them "Yeah I got an old horse. Clarence is out there working him right now if you're interested." They looked across the field and watched Clarence make a couple turns, Zeb said "I got to warn you, though, the old horse don't look good."

Daddy told him he didn't care anything about how the horse looked, so he and Zeb struck a deal and Barney loaded the horse.

The next morning Daddy and Barney hit the fields early. It wasn't long before Daddy noticed that Barney was plowing up more corn than weeds, so he waited at the end of his row for Barney to catch up. Barney stopped the old horse and walked around to the front, he waved his hands at the horse's eyes and said, "Mr. Claud, that man was right, this horse don't look good. In fact he don't look at all he's blind as a bat".

At the end of the summer, after harvest, Barney left us. He didn't say a word to anyone, he just didn't show up for breakfast. Mama told Daddy that she wished she had known he was leaving, she would have packed him some old clothes. Daddy said "Don't worry about it he would have told you to give them to some poor person anyway". Barney had his pride.

A close friend of mine works at the homeless shelter in Charlotte when he has the time. He told me recently about a young man he met there who was down on his luck. Max found out that he was a heavy equipment operator, but couldn't find a job. In Max's business, he is in contact with Utility Contractors regularly. He made a few calls and set up an appointment for the young man. As far as I know the man is still working everyday and doesn't need the shelter anymore. All it took was someone to care.

As you spend your time on the corporate ladder and it seems that you're not getting anywhere, reach down instead of up. For every step that you lift someone, it elevates you two. And remember, like Jake and Barney, the person you're helping has just as much pride as you have.

Mike A. Marr, Sr.

Spiders and Other Critters

I've been accused of single-handedly ending the Lake Wylie real estate boom, causing otherwise normal people to lock their doors and windows and cower in the corners of their living rooms and making grown men check under their beds before going to sleep. All because of a few little snakes I may have mentioned. HEY! It was a joke. There are no Hoop snakes, there are no Joint snakes, there are no Copperheads, oh wait, maybe there are Copperheads.

Mrs. Grace Alexander informed me that people in River Hills were all locking their doors and staying home for fear of stepping on a snake. The Realty Industry is convinced that my snake article is responsible for the decline in housing sales, no one wants to live amongst snakes.

There are snakes in the Lake Wylie area, but no more than you will find anywhere else. These snakes like nothing more than to be left alone, and will not bother anyone who doesn't bother them. I apologize for any hysteria I may have caused and am truly sorry for any undue stress generated in the reading public.

Snakes are our friends and you should not fear them, but respect them. Let me tell you what you should fear, insects. Insects are a different story.

People just don't understand how powerful the Realty Cartel is in this area. Remember the Mexican Killer Bees and how they were only a few states away from us and bearing down. That was five years ago. I think the story is being suppressed because those bees are probably in Lamar, SC right now and waiting for the right time to attack.

The same can be said for fireants. We lived in Summerville, SC in the early '80s and they were everywhere down there. Our back yard was full of ant mounds, but Diane, being the resourceful person she is, figured out how to get rid of them. She took the lawn mower and leveled every pile, barefooted. After treating over 3000 bites, she decided that maybe those mounds didn't look so bad. Have you heard any News lately about fireants? I don't think so.

Mosquitoes in Lake Wylie are bigger than anywhere else on Earth. I heard a fisherman tell the story of two large mosquitoes on

Hero of Bullfrog Hill

Mill creek that were checking him out. One said, "He looks like a tasty morsel". To which the other replied, "Yea, but we better take him with us or the big ones will take him away from us."

There are other insects that don't even have names yet, some of them fly, some crawl and some just slither around under the bed. All, however, are more dangerous than snakes.

Spiders, though they are technically arachnids instead of insects, are the worst. Some people will tell you there are no spiders in their yards, but this is easy to disprove. As a child, I learned to hunt spiders. On a dark evening, place the back end of a flashlight against your forehead, just over and between your eyes. Get down on your hands and knees and shine the light across the lawn about ten feet in front of you. All those little sparkling jewels in the grass are spider eyes staring back at you. I will assure those naysayers mentioned above that their immaculate yards are filled with thousands of spiders eyes. Where there are eyes, there are spiders.

Floyd McCarter told me recently of a huge hairy spider he saw in his garage. It was lurking underneath his wife's car and was the size of a small kitten. After killing it, he realized that it must have given birth to thousands of its own kind. He may move to Kansas.

In our own yard, we are visited each summer by the infamous writing spider. His web is three to four feet across and he spends his time crisscrossing the web with silk, sometimes actually spelling words. My Grandmother always warned me to stay away from the writing spider's web, because if he happened to spell your name, you would die before morning.

The Black Widow is probably the most popular spider in the Carolinas and may be found in practically every household. With a red hourglass design on its abdomen and a shiny black coat, it is the most beautiful of spiders and the most gruesome. After mating, the female eats the male. Talk about commitment on the male's part.

Another very poisonous spider is the Brown Recluse. She is called that because she stays in out of the way places like that lingerie drawer that seldom gets opened or behind the trophies on the top shelf that never get dusted.

Mike A. Marr, Sr.

Years ago, Mose Andy was found dead in his shack. The records say that he drank himself to death, but no one ever explained why his body was wrapped tightly in spider webs.

As you read this, look around and notice the cobwebs up there in the corner and remember, there is something up there that made that web, looking back at you, WAITING.

Where is Spenser?

I came home the other day and parked the truck in the usual spot. I turned off the engine and opened the door in the usual way and there in my lap was the head of a black and white Border collie looking up at me in an unusual way. Farley had a sad look in his eyes like he was lost. I rubbed behind his ears and asked how he had been and then asked where his partner in crime was off to, in the usual way. Spenser was nowhere to be found or heard.

He always takes off for the woods when I pull in the driveway and pretends that he is the great hunter. You can hear this deep hoarse baying coming from somewhere down by the creek and are expected to believe that he has treed the biggest raccoon in Lake Wylie. He will show up later soaking wet and want to be petted for being such a good hunting dog.

Spenser (with an S, like the poet) came to us as part of the package when Arnie moved back home a few years ago. He had always been kept on a leash or inside an invisible fence and found that the two to three hundred acres behind us was the Heaven he had always looked for. Arnie, our resident English major named him and I never was sure whether he was named for the poet or for Robert Parker's private investigator. If anything he should have been named Hawk for Spenser's big black muscular sidekick.

He ruled the roost around here from day one, keeping Diane's cats on their toes and all the ferocious neighbor dogs out of his yard. He minded well enough and understood the commands "Sit", "Stay" and "Down", as long as it suited him to entertain you. When something else caught his attention he was off and running and all the yelling in the world couldn't stop him.

Spenser had arthritis in his hindquarters and would drag one leg. I remember one night when we were watching the comet he moved from one to another staying just long enough to get his ears rubbed. He could barely get around he was hurting so badly, but he loved all the attention. When something moved at the edge of the field, he was gone like a flash of lightning and returned a few minutes later with a possum in his mouth, all the pain forgotten.

When Arnie moved out again we inherited the big Lab and he and Farley were inseparable. They chased the meter man together, they barked at the UPS driver and they kept the mail lady from her appointed rounds. We always knew when someone pulled in the driveway and when an ambulance would be coming up the road. Spenser could hear the siren two minutes before any human and would let out a bloodcurdling howl. Farley howled too but he never knew why. He is for all practical purposes as deaf as a bedpost.

When I finally got past Farley and into the house Diane told me that Spenser hadn't eaten anything the night before and had left most of his food since the weekend. We decided that we needed to find him and went to the woods calling his name. Farley was right there with us and still looked like someone had licked all the red off his candy. We didn't find Spenser in the woods and as we got back to the house Diane saw him under the back deck.

She said, "I can't tell if he is moving."

I could tell. He wasn't. Spenser died in a dignified manner with his front legs crossed and his head to one side as if he had just gone to sleep. I pulled him out from under the deck and wrapped him in a sheet. His favorite pastime was to sleep in the Iris bed even though he knew it irked me immensely. Spenser is now spending eternity in the Iris bed. I'm really going to miss that old dog.

Something in the Water

Word on the street is that a new resident has moved into the Lake Wylie area and there is no welcome wagon to greet him. According to the Newspaper our new friend is not native to this region and therefore should be captured and sent on his way. Well, isn't that a unique way to treat newcomers. I'm talking about the alligator of course not any taxpayer.

My first close encounter with a gator happened about ten years ago on beautiful Bald Head Island. I was playing golf with the utility manager and we were hitting our second shot on the eleventh or twelfth hole, a long par four with water all the way down the right hand side. Across the small lagoon an ibis had entangled itself in some fishing line and was hanging about six feet above the surface from a small tree thrashing wildly. Dave stopped the cart a few feet away and said "Watch this".

Swimming leisurely toward the helpless bird was a seven-foot alligator with a grin on his face. I looked at Dave and said, "He won't be able to reach it" to which he replied "He won't have the chance". The gator stopped grinning and retreated at triple his original speed. I looked at Dave questioningly and noticed the same sly smile the gator had recently had.

The ibis stopped thrashing and I'll swear I heard it utter the term "Uh Oh". The placid pond exploded right beneath the bird and in an instant the ibis, fishing line and limb were all gone. I saw for just a second why the other gator was running away and it was an awesome sight. My round of golf fell apart as I cautiously watched every bush and mud hole for the rest of the day.

Dave told me later that the last decent measurement they had of Milly, she was over seventeen feet long and posed no danger to the local residents. I asked him if all the golfers checked in and out at the clubhouse so they could be sure she wasn't feeding. He just laughed.

Alligators are not new to Lake Wylie. When I was just a kid a friend of Daddy's kept one in the pond behind his house. Her name was Sally and she was known to snag stray dogs that stopped by for a quick drink. Mr. Bill fed here live chickens and soup bones. I remember going to his house one summer and he was all excited and hurried us to his greenhouse. He had collected eggs Sally had laid and they had hatched the night before. There were several small alligators in a box snapping at anything that moved. Bill said they reminded him of Sally when he had bought her in Florida. Now, I'm no lizard expert but I'm pretty sure there needs to be a father. Sally was the only gator living in Mr. Bill's pond so where did the mate come from?

There are a few known cases of locals raising gators and releasing them but I would get into trouble if I mentioned any names here. You know who you are. Some of these animals had some size on them. I'm not suggesting that our new friend is one of these but you never know.

Maybe he's not alone, maybe there is a whole colony of alligators and this is just the first one anyone has seen. Some creatures when moving to new areas like to keep pretty much to themselves. It was years before River Hills residents came out at night and now many are respected members of our society.

Why don't we just leave ol' Wylie Gator alone and see what he is up to. He has probably read all the complaints about muskrats and geese and figures Lake Wylie would be a good place to retire.

Snakes Revisited

> We were strolling through the park one day
> In the merry merry month of May.
> When out of the lake crawled a big ugly snake
> And we ran all the rest of the way.

That's right, May is here and snake season can't be far behind. I remember seeing snakes as a kid but they stayed in the woods out of the way of people and people stayed out of the woods where the snakes lived. Today, however, people are building their houses in the very woods where those snakes have dwelt for years. Is it any wonder they are upset?

Snakes can turn up in the strangest places. My sister-in-law called a few years ago and wanted someone to come help get a snake out of her underwear drawer. Libby was the perfect choice since she was the only one not afraid of snakes. Some say that's because she is meaner than they are. She caught the little critter behind the neck and shook it at the rest of us as she took it back outside. She only got bitten a little bit.

When I was five, Dewitt was building a new house. There was a sand pile out front used to mix mortar for the brickwork. It looked like the perfect place to play especially with the little soft marbles I found buried there. I got scared when they started moving on their own and then the babies came out. Did you know that baby copperheads are just as dangerous as the adults?

The riverbanks have their own special kind of snakes called cottonmouth moccasins. I have always been told that they can't bite under water but I can, fish can, and birds can so I don't really believe that. I was playing along the edge of Mill Creek one day and had just climbed down from a tree when I heard something above me. I looked up just in time to see a rather large moccasin slither down the same tree and plop into the water. From then on I checked all trees carefully before climbing them.

Daddy always kept a black snake in the barn to keep the rats under control. That thing would get up in the rafters and lay in wait. Sometimes when feeding up I would see it up there with a big bulge in its stomach wrapping itself tightly around a beam and squeezing the life out its poor victim. One day about two feet of it was hanging down when I walked in. It looked me straight in the eye as if to say, "You're next". I was always careful to locate that old snake after that.

Snake Burton and some other guys were going frog gigging one night and asked if I would like to come along. I agreed and we pushed off in the small boat. We hadn't gone far when he saw two beady eyes in the flashlight beam and rammed the gig right between them. When he pulled it into the boat, it was the longest frog I had ever seen. The boat emptied quickly and we went back the next day to see if old no shoulders would give our boat back.

I don't see as many snakes these days as I did back then but I haven't heard anything about a decrease in the serpent population either. With all the construction going on in Lake Wylie there are fewer wooded areas for them to live naturally so I can only assume that they are adapting to the new conditions. Debra had lived in the edge of the woods when that one climbed in her drawer. Maybe he told his friends that people are not all that bad after all and they could probably live in perfect harmony with us if they stayed out of the way.

If I were you I would be careful opening drawers and digging in the flowerbeds. I wouldn't park my convertible under any trees either. That little pile of sand left over from construction; make sure the kids don't play with the soft white marbles. And do I even need to mention the Anacondas released by the Government over in Albemarle County? Those things are migratory you know.

A Little Southern Reading

I was in the CVS the other day picking up some odds and ends when on the book display I noticed John Jake's new book, *On Secret Service*. I knew we were going to the beach and I would need something to read so I picked it up. I had listened to the first few chapters on public radio but had gotten out of range and lost my place.

As I was checking out an alarm of some kind went off and everyone ignored it as we in the South always do. Everyone, that is except the little lady behind me. She was as nervous as a fox in the dog pound. "What is that?" she asked, "Isn't anyone going to do something?"

As you know we think of alarms as a nuisance invented by people from up north to annoy us and went on with our business. Finally, the lady behind the counter explained that someone had probably opened the back door. "Well", the nervous lady started, "The manager was here just a minute ago. Maybe he went out. I'm sure the police will be here soon."

I just smiled at the checkout lady and placed my few items on the counter. That's when she noticed my book. "Oh", she said, "John Jakes, I'll have to go to the library and check it out", she finished with an air of superiority. I started to tell her I would buy her a copy if she couldn't afford it. But I didn't.

"What's it about?" she asked.

I explained, "It's about the Secret Service", and then as delicately as possible continued, "during the recent unpleasantness. You know, The War Between the States."

She raised her hackles and said, "I know what you mean, I'm a Yankee and proud of it."

I started to tell her God had afflicted all of us with some burden. I had a bad case of hemorrhoids but I wasn't bragging about it. But I didn't. I started to ask if she was so proud when was she going back there. But I didn't. I just said, "I'm sorry", at which the checkout lady smiled again.

She then said, "At least we don't have grits, yuck."

I couldn't help myself, she had gotten personal. I asked, "You don't like grits?"

Mike A. Marr, Sr.

"No", she shuddered, "They taste like fish eyeballs cooked in motor oil."

I just shook my head. I couldn't argue with her because I have never eaten fish eyeballs cooked in motor oil but I assume that in Yankee country it is considered a delicacy. Yankees will eat some strange things. I once ate lunch with a Yankee who poured pancake syrup on his grits. I guess it reminded him of that motor oil stuff the lady was talking about.

Can anyone out there tell me why the farther north you travel, the harder the dinner rolls are? We ate dinner in New York once and the bread was so hard I wouldn't have fed it to my dog much less put it on the table for guest to try to eat. I bent my butter knife trying to get it open.

They cook their vegetables funny, too. Their green beans are crunchy and they cook their tomatoes. Some of them, I have been told, even eat eggplant. I ordered a hotdog all the way and they put sauerkraut on it.

This Yankee invasion all started in 1954 when one of our fine Southern Belles went off to New York to seek her fortune. What she found instead was Neil Driscoll and eventually brought him back here. Neil, the self-proclaimed Harbormaster of Lake Wylie tells the story one way but I'm sure Gail has a different version. I haven't had a chance to ask her about it, yet.

I don't know what the alarm was about and I really don't care. I don't know what happened to the little Yankee lady and I really don't care. I did read the book and suggest that you save your money and check it out at the library. I don't want to give away the ending but the South lost again. I think John Jakes must be a Yankee sympathizer.

South-Speak

"Squoeet"
"Wurgahneet?"
"Dawno, McDonald's, If yeontu?"
"Umigimacote".

Translation:
"Let's go eat".
"Where are you going to eat?"
"I don't Know, McDonald's, If you want to?"
"Let me get my coat."

Occasionally, people from other parts of the World have a hard time understanding folks from the South. The problem arises from the pronunciation of vowels. Southerner's love vowels and stretch them out to their full extent, while skipping over several of the nonmusical consonants. Up North, consonants rule, while vowels are just in the way and if they are pronounced at all, they are squished to practical nonexistence.

In "1984" (the book not the year), George Orwell introduced New-speak, a language to save time during News broadcasts. Orwell, being British, probably never visited the South or he would have known that New-speak couldn't catch on.

Southerner's like the sound of words and use as many as possible to express themselves. Ya'll is a perfect example of a good Southern word. It looks simple enough, but is actually pronounced in two distinct syllables, ye and all. There are other examples of South-speak and I'll try to lead you through some of them.

Sometimes, the problem is with the use of certain words. Diane is constantly going potty. If you look potty up in the dictionary, you will find that it is equivalent to losing your mind. Some of you may know Diane and agree with this definition, but I know better She is just going to the restroom and I know she goes potty several times a day.

Sometimes terms fall out of use for reasons that are too obvious. Take Dope, during my lifetime, I have downed many dopes, but am afraid to order one anymore. A dope can represent many different manufacturers. There are Pepsi dopes, Coke dopes and the one the term probably derived from, Double Cola dopes. As I said, dope has fallen on hard times, mainly because you can't find Double Colas these days.

Won't is another strictly Southern term. I know, I know, won't is the contraction of will not as in "I won't be home for supper". In South-speak, however it is also interchangeable with 'was not' and 'were not'. "They won't no where near there when the fire started". "Tom won't there neither". I promise I won't go any further with won't.

My son works with a young Oriental gentleman who is not only learning English but is also trying to master South-speak. One term he has picked up is "House ya Momma an nem?" a greeting used commonly to inquire about a person's family. The Oriental twist to it does have an unusual ring, "House yo Mumma (pause) and dam?" The New Jersey born sales manager is still clueless.

Sometimes a word just travels in different circles. I heard recently about a lady who was told to go down the dirt road and then turn right at the white doublewide. Not wanting to sound ignorant, she rode up and down that road for hours trying to figure out what a doublewide looks like. It's a mobile home lady, something now on the endangered species list in York County.

Fixin, as in I'm fixin to finish up here, is also quite Southern. Life in the South is so slow that you can't just do something, you have to get ready first. In a fight, one participant may say 'I'm fixin to bust you up real good", the other may reply, "Gee eet yit?" To which the first would say "Yeontu?" and off they would go to McDonald's, both fixin to get sumpin' good.

They Tore Down The Mustang

We went to Myrtle Beach the weekend before Easter. That place has changed a bit since the '60s and '70s when we went every summer. Lake Arrowhead, where we camped is now Kingston Plantation, a conglomeration of condos. The bypass no longer does, it's just as busy as Ocean Drive. There are places to eat like *Planet Hollywood, The Nascar Café* and *The Hardrock Café*. Can someone explain to me what any of these have to do with the ocean or surfing or sunbathing or even fishing?

For those of you who are interested, Arnie and Angie came in fifth at Duck's in the amateur division. They really didn't expect to place since it was their first shag competition. We got to meet Jackie and Charlie Friday night. They are just plain old folks.

Saturday, we drove down Ocean Drive and tried to remember the motels where we had stayed. I always thought the Diplomat and the Florentine were the high-class joints but not anymore, they are just small motels amid the giants that block out the sun. The dunes have left and there is nothing protecting the many swimming pools from the surf. Even the sand has changed, what sand you could find. I am really sorry Myrtle Beach but you are not what you used to be.

I looked at the uncontrolled growth and wondered what Lake Wylie might be like in ten years. It will not be a very pretty sight. Most of the people who moved in here and changed everything to the way it was wherever they moved from, have now moved on to disrupt some other small community. Why is it that people move to the country and then complain about it being country? They complain because there are no grocery stores. Well, we now have two huge ones. They complain because there is nowhere to go out to eat. Take your choice, McDonald's, Burger King and now Wendy's have all moved into the area.

I know that I sound a little upset but in case you haven't noticed someone has torn down the Mustang, the very last vestige of the life I once knew. Is nothing sacred anymore? For years the Mustang was the home of the best Cheeseburger in Lake Wylie. Now all you can get are cardboard cheeseburgers from one of the fast-food places. And how do they make those French-fries taste that bad? They always ask if you want to upsize, Hell, I can barely eat what they give me.

Joe's Fish Camp is gone, Capt' Lyle's is gone, even the Hungry Fisherman is gone. There is nowhere in Lake Wylie to get fish anymore. You would think that a lake would have a fish camp.

We seldom go to Myrtle Beach because of all the changes that have been made. I guess the time is coming to leave Lake Wylie behind as well. Maybe we can move to Hickory Grove, I understand that the Yankees haven't found it, yet. The problem with Hickory Grove is that there are no grocery stores and there really isn't a good place to eat. Besides, Diane and I both grew up here so we will just have to put up with all the nonsense.

One thing is for sure, though, when they decide to tear out the dam because they need the lake bottom for housing, I am out of here.

Southern Lexicon

Sometimes, you will hear something that reminds you of the age-old battle between environment and genetics. During the Olympics, a friend of mine said he sure was glad that he hadn't been born in Japan. When asked why, he replied that he didn't speak a word of Japanese and would have a hard time getting along. That's environment. There was also the story about the lady who took her small portable TV to Nagano to keep up with her soaps. She just knew that the TVs over there would all be in Japanese and she wouldn't be able to understand them. That's genetics.

I'm not sure which has the most influence on people, but I am sure that environment does have an effect on how we communicate and about this time each year, important to point out some of the differences between northern and southern speech. The following is a list of words and phrases used in the South that may be helpful to our new northern friends as they go through the period of adjustment to Southern life.

Arsh—This is not what you think, you're thinking about arse which is the South end of a mule heading North. Arsh is a type of tater. In the South, you put an arsh tater in your pintos as they're cooking to soak up the gas that is usually released in other ways.

Warsh—This is what you do to the arsh tater before putting it in the crock-pot, it removes all the dirt and the loose eyes. You can also warsh the human body but that requires a special cloth called a warsh rag.

Wont—There are several meanings and a few different spellings of this word. Johnny's Mother asked, "You wont some more pintos?" But everyone knew Johnny wont likely to eat no pintos for supper, cause he had a big date and didn't rightly trust the arsh tater.

Ratcheer—A term to describe a location. You ask a local where they were born and they are likely to answer "Ratcheer"

Dowhut—The proper Southern term for "huh" meaning "Would you run that by again, I didn't quite catch it all" a variation used when names are involved would be "Shot who?"

Thasnise—A term you can slip into a boring conversation when you are not really paying attention. A few people will know the real meaning of this word but we can't go into that here.

Redneck—A term of endearment for a brother or uncle or other loved one meaning just a little bit country. The backwoodsmen in the movie *Deliverance* were not rednecks, they were just plain mean.

Mite—A diminutive adjective usually used sarcastically to mean a small amount. The backwoodsmen in *Deliverance* were a mite unfriendly.

Hash it out—If you have a problem with one of your Redneck friends and need to discuss it with him, you may go over to his house and hash it out.

Went upside his head—Means you hit him pretty good.

Den—What happens next. Me and Johnny were hashing it out, den I went upside his head to get my point across.

Uncrunk—Also used interchangeably, cranked down. This is what happens to your car when it cuts off. "Joanie was in heavy traffic when her car came uncrunk."

Raise the window down—This is 'what you do when your car comes uncrunk in traffic, so you can holler at somebody to send help.

Hero of Bullfrog Hill

Cold heat—When you first crank your car in the morning and turn the heater on too soon, that's the kind of air that comes through the vents.

Goodern—The type of joke that makes you reach down and slap your knee.

Sistern—A term you use when you mean more than just your sister, as in "My sistern her husband came by the other day to hash it out. I immediately went upside his head."

Squish—An activity performed barefooted after a summer rainstorm. You squish the mud between your toes.

Look the mail—What you do around lunchtime to see if the Sear's catalog has come yet.

Landsake—You have to remember that for most Southerners, the land is the most important thing there is, they're not making any more of it. Anything for the sake of the land is truly important.

As you can see, a lot of Sou'speak is contraction. We can contract anything "ern" is a good example. It is the contraction of "er" and "than" and can be added to the end of most adjectives to make a 'whole new word. "He was lazyern a hound dog in the noonday sun." "His date was biggern a WCW wrestler."

There are also some terms you need to avoid when you move South. As a part of my research, I have slipped the word skosh into conversation recently and always get the same result. "Dowhut". We just don't get it. You should also avoid 'On the lam', someone may think you have found out about their redneck Uncle's latest affair and take offense. As you're laying In the hospital, you'll want to know 'why they went upside your head.

I trust this small lexicon will help some of our northern friends with their transition and prevent a few embarrassing moments in the new Winn-Dixie as they come into contact with the local Southern dialects. Remember, If someone says something and you don't quite get it, proper etiquette requires that you look them straight in the face and say "Dowhut".

How They Did It Up North?

At a recent Shag Club meeting I had the opportunity to chat with a very dear friend who suffered through no fault of her own from that tragic misfortune of being born above the Mason-Dixon Line. Yes, there are Yankee shaggers and some of them are nice people. Jay and Connie saw the light and moved south several years ago and joined the shaggers shortly thereafter.

Connie was telling me that she had been following with some interest an editorial response that I had sent into the Herald and was surprised at how it had generated even more responses. The whole thing started when a gentleman from Detroit had complained about the traffic lights in Rock Hill and explained how much better they were up north. I simply pointed out to him that he came here by choice and could go back up there very quickly via United Airlines. It seems that everyone had two cents worth that they wanted to add concerning his dilemma.

Poor Connie saw this as a verbal assault in the continuing battle between North and South and wondered why that battle rages on nearly one hundred fifty years later. What she doesn't realize is the battle is so much older than just one hundred and fifty years.

If you go back to 1776 you will find a group of people who were very upset about Great Britain trying to tell them how to do things. These people revolted and headed up their army with George Washington, a southerner from Virginia. Sure, Ben Franklin, John Adams and some others were also involved but they weren't the first President were they? Washington whipped old King George with the help of some southerners who kept Cornwallis from advancing northward. The poor British General complained constantly because the rebels wouldn't fight properly. They just wouldn't do it like the British used to do it back home.

Most true southerners are of Scotch-Irish descent and if you go back even further to the 14th century you find that they were having problems with England even then. Of course they were the northerners at that time but the English were trying to tell them how to do things and they took offense. That revolt led to Scotland's independence from Great Britain.

Mike A. Marr, Sr.

    I'm fairly sure that even the Celts and the Picts were revolting from someone or else they would never have ended up in Scotland and Ireland in the first place.

    Janice and Floyd are also Shag Club members and moved down here from Maryland a few years back. They have had some problems acclimating to the southern lifestyle, also but as I have explained to Floyd on several occasions Maryland is below the M-D Line and he is a true southerner. He always comes back with, "Well, you are the first one to notice."

    The point I tried to make with Connie is that we don't mind you coming down here and learning our ways. We don't mind you talking funny. We don't mind that you had a better way of doing things up north. We just don't want to hear about it. We don't care.

Yankee Spies

About a year ago I did an article about Southern speech and got a complaint from a so-called Southerner who thought I was making fun of him. He accused me of being from north of the Mason-Dixon line. Let me assure you that I was born and raised right here in Dear Ol' Bethel and Dear Ol' Bethel is about as Southern as one can get.

The article mentioned was actually meant to help our northern friends cope with life in the South and to help them understand our ways so that they might fit in. What I didn't realize at the time was that most of them don't want to fit in, they want things to be like they were back home. If things were so great back home, why are they down here bothering us?

A friend of mine recently mentioned a bumper sticker he was thinking of putting on his car. The caption "North 1, South 0, Halftime" tells more about southern attitudes than anything I have seen lately. If you don't like the flag of the Confederacy flying over the State Capitol, go away. There are forty-nine other states that don't have it.

Folks, we are being infiltrated by northern spies. I read recently that sixty thousand New Yorkers have moved to our fair state. Either they didn't know about our flag or they are here to tear it down. South Carolina was the first state to secede from the Union last time but with enough Yankees living here the next vote may go the other way. We may end up as the Southern headquarters for the whole Yankee army.

Jeff Foxworthy, a true Son of the South, made a career out of poking fun at rednecks even though he probably was one. His term "You might be a redneck if..." is recognized and used by everyone. Now anyone can spot a redneck a mile away. Jeff and I have both inadvertently given the Yankees clues on how to be Southern and it is now time to try to correct that huge mistake by pointing out "You might be a Yankee if..."

You have ever played boil in the yawd.
You think suck tail and eat head is a bad thing.
You think beach music has anything to do with Brian Wilson.
You have ever paid someone to see a snake.

You have ever defiled your grits with maple syrup.

You have ever gone to SOS and did something called Hand Dancing.

You have ever used the term youse guys to identify a group of people.

You think a Dodge mini-van is a high performance vehicle.

And finally, if you have ever said, "That's not the way we do it back home." You might be a Yankee.

My friends it is up to us to locate these Yankees and keep an eye on them. You can tell them by their actions and their words. They are trying hard to fit in with the rest of us but their heritage belies them and they will give themselves away every time. Just when you think you have converted one, you go by their house and there they are cheering for Michigan or Ohio State or some other foreign school and you'll know where their true allegiance lies.

Bill Ingvall, another Son of the South, has suggested that we hand out signs to stupid people so we don't get aggravated when they do something natural. Our real estate salespeople have the first contact with these Yankee spies and it seems they could provide them with some kind of pin that would let the rest of us know. Maybe, they are actually Yankee sympathizers or the all mighty dollar has clouded their eyes. Remember youse guys, carpetbaggers always spread a lot of money around just before they take over the plantation.

Prejudice

Okay, I admit it, I'm one of those prejudiced people you have heard so much about. There is one group that I definitely have a big problem sharing my time and energy with. They don't mean to be that way it's just the way they were raised. The problem is they are raising their kids to be just like them. I don't even think it is premeditated. It is just the way they talk and act. Little things they say are picked up by the kids who repeat it and the parents think it is cute.

On a recent visit to a small southern church I shook hands with the minister who promptly told me the following. "This black man (he used the other word) applied for a job at the police station. The desk Sargent said he would have to take a test first and asked him, 'What is 1 and 1?' The man thought for a minute and answered, 'That gotta be leben'. The Sargent said, 'Well, yeah, I guess it could be eleven. Now what is 4 and 4?' He thought again and said, 'That be fo-t-fo.' The Sargent said, 'It could be forty-four. One last question, who killed Abraham Lincoln?' The man said, 'Well sir, I really don't know.' The Sargent told him to go home and work on it.

When he got home his wife asked how things went and he told her, 'It must have gone pretty good, they already got me working on a murder case.'"

Why couldn't the man have been Jewish, Irish Italian or even Southern Baptist? Maybe he could be a Televangelist, now that would be funny. If the preacher is telling that kind of joke in public, what in the world is preaching from the pulpit? I told him one of my cleaner dirty jokes to see if he would flinch like I just had. It had no effect so I moved away quickly. Yes, I am prejudiced. I really don't like being in close proximity to bigots.

Ethnic jokes of any kind are cruel to someone and there is no place for them in our modern society. As adults we have a responsibility to help our children understand the world in which they have to live. Stereotyping certain groups does nothing to improve their ability to get along.

This goes for blacks as well as whites. I have heard some of you call someone an "Uncle Tom" because he is obsequious (look it up). I would suggest that you read the book beforehand you might decide that you are actually paying him a compliment. Uncle Tom was a fairly strong character.

I do have one problem with blacks. That is their ability to really tic me off on the Interstate. Not all of them are bad drivers, just the women who are over thirty years old and fifty pounds over weight. Ladies, who told you to drive in the passing lane?

There is now a new ethnic group moving into our area. Hispanics are the fastest growing population unit in South Carolina. Do we now ask how many Mexicans it takes to screw in a light bulb? It probably doesn't take but one, they are hard workers you know.

When we were just kids we all told little moron jokes. I was a teenager before I knew what moron meant and by then I thought my friends who were telling the jokes fit the description to a T. Maybe we should all start telling Kiwi jokes, I don't know of any New Zealanders living close by. Besides, they are a laid back kind of people who probably wouldn't mind anyway.

My one big concern for that preacher is what will he think when he gets to heaven and discovers that God is a black woman who drives in the left hand lane.

Don't Call at Suppertime

Pitney-Bowes called last week and didn't ask about my mail service, they wanted to be my credit card company. When the mail arrived, AT&T was offering me a $20,000 credit limit to sign up with their MasterCard. Then, I opened a letter from SC Farm Bureau, my home insurance carrier, and lo and behold they wanted me to open a bank account with them and receive a Platinum Visa. American Express, the only credit card I use, now wants to sell me insurance. People, what's wrong with doing what you are paid to do? Why is everyone trying to get into everyone else's business?

I think it all started a few years ago with K-Mart. I was sitting around the house watching a little football on a perfect Saturday afternoon when the phone rings. Like an idiot I answer it just as Notre Dame is about to get scored on again and someone from K-Mart wants me to take a survey. If I agree to answer a few questions they will send me a gift certificate for $25.00. UCLA has the game well in hand so I tell him to start talking. Where do I buy groceries? At the grocery store. Where do I get my prescriptions filled? At the drugstore. Where do I buy my tires? At the tire store. This type of questioning continued for some time before he hit me with the zinger. Would I be interested in a Superstore that sold all these products and many more besides? My answer must have been wrong because I never got that gift certificate and haven't been back to K-Mart since.

Diane likes to shop at the Wal-Mart in York but I have a problem with buying clothes, food and getting an oil change all under one roof. There is an old saying about Jack of all trades and master of none that I firmly believe in, do one thing and do it well. Anyone who tries to be everything to everyone is shortchanging someone.

It can't be too long before McDonald's becomes a true drive-thru. You will pull into the store, get a McHaircut and enjoy a steaming plate of McSketty while your car is getting a McOilchange and a McWash.

Someday soon, Town will be one giant store where you buy everything you could possibly ever need and then carry it all to a checkout line where some youngster will have to get a price check on your football tickets. Maybe they will just have the game there in a big central arena where they could also have concerts and conventions.

Call me old fashioned but I like going to Harry's to pick up a couple of screws and some screen wire. I like going to Jac-Lynn's to buy birthday cards. I like going to Lake Wylie Photo to get my pictures developed. I like grocery stores to have groceries and drugstores to have drugs. I like my telephone company to provide telephone service and I like my insurance company to stick to insurance.

I like my life pretty much the way it is and if I want to change anything I'll call you. So stop ruining my Saturdays by calling in the middle of a football game and stop calling in the middle of my supper. I have found one good way to annoy telemarketers that seems to work well. When one calls and starts their spiel I simply lay the phone down and go back to whatever I was doing before. Once they think they have your attention they will give their entire sales pitch. You may want to pick it up and say uhuh ever so often. After five or ten minutes the phone gives that irritating off hook signal and I hang it up. Not only do I not have to listen to their drivel but also I like to think that I have saved at least one other person from these dinnertime predators.

Maybe I am being a little too critical. I have my own company and I guess I could stand to diversify. How about it, anyone out there need insurance, long distance service, a Visa or even a cheeseburger? Call me and let's do lunch. Oh, wait, I'm supposed to call you. Would you rather I call on Saturday or is suppertime better for you?

More Southernisms

I was chastised for getting uppity not long ago by a very good friend. She said I had gotten above my raising. Gale isn't right very often but this time I have to agree with her. I used the term "guest" in an article. I apologize for that. Here in the south we don't have guest, we don't have guest rooms and we don't have guest towels we have company who stay in the spare bedroom and use the good towels. I blame this lapse on the northerners that have moved into our community. Their ways are encroaching on the best of us.

With that in mind and the fact that school is starting it is probably a good time to recap some southernisms for these folks. In southern speech we use contractions just like they do up north but we also use something that I call confractions. A contraction puts two or more words together by dropping a letter or so and using an apostrophe. With a confraction you may not even end up in the same part of the alphabet.

Chu (pronounced like duh) is a confraction. It not only replaces several words but can be used in different ways to replace completely different words.

"Chu doing?" What are you doing?

"Chu do on that test?" How did you do on that test?

Now some people may think that we are lazy. That's not true we are just considerably conservative. They think we talk slowly when actually they are processing what we say slowly. With so many new northern teachers and pupils in our schools there are some other words that they will need to know to understand the locals.

Annim: refers to all one's close relatives, uncles, aunts, brothers, sisters and the cousins that are still claimed. "How's your momma annim?"

Nuglian: refers to the fact that something isn't pretty. When asked, "Chu think of my new dog?" You reply, "She's a nuglian". To which they may answer, "Purdimuch but she zakeeper".

Mike A. Marr, Sr.

Fixinto: what you say when you haven't done something quite yet. "I'm fixinto go to town chu need anything?"

Lybulda: what you say when something might happen but hasn't yet. "That dog's lybulda to bite you."

Pestern: when someone is bothering you. "Teacher, Billy keeps pestern me."

Addle: another confraction of that will. "Addle do it".

Disseanin: that particular time of day right after supper. "What ya'll doing disseanin?"

Dadayuhdamar: this is when someone is fixinto do something. "I'll get around to it either dadayuhdamar."

I trust this will help our northern company to fit in just a little better and maybe understand us. All it takes is a little figurin' on their part and things will be fine. I don't want any of ya'll writing letters to the editor complaining about me making fun of southerners either. Let me 'splain something to ya'll. I was born here, raised here and have lived here all my life. My momma annim talk like this and nobody makes fun of my momma.

SECTION III

LIVING SOUTHERN STYLE

Living in the south requires a moderate amount of toleration. The hardest part is watching things change right in front of your eyes. I have noticed that I have started saying "Back in my day."

Mike A. Marr, Sr.

To Kill a Mocking Bird

Ah! The arrival of spring, with grass to cut, shrubs to trim and undergrowth to cut back, makes a person happy to live in the country. Did I say something about undergrowth? Well, that reminds me of 1970 and a new development taking form down on Lake Wylie. It was called River Hills Plantation and would be built around Joe's Fish Camp. I was working for Maw Bell, but had just lost my driving license for having a heavy foot and needing a job close to home, I decided to check it out. There were many locals already working for the Fraisers, and I took a position clearing lots and setting corner posts for the new project.

Jack Nichols, Gary Neal, Harry Sadler and I, along with several others were handed bushaxes, chainsaws, and doublebits and dumped on Fairway Ridge. Our direction was to clear the lots so that standing at one corner, you could see the other three. We started in earnest on lot #1 and cut every tree smaller than our leg. By the end of the first week, we had cleared over ten lots and were quite proud of ourselves. That's when the Salesmen started showing up with all kinds of suggestions about how we should do what we were doing.

People were paying up to $8000.00 for one of these lots and they wanted them to look like country. We had all grown up in the country and knew what country looked like, which caused a dilemma. Why would anyone pay that much money for a half-acre lot and what did Cityfolk think country looked like?

Our problem was solved by a fine old gentleman that many of you may remember. Mr. Walt Colvin showed up and told us not to cut any Dogwoods, Cedar, or Curly Maple. Well, if you know anything about this area, you know that all the underbrush is either Dogwood, Cedar, or Curly Maple. Having cut down on our workload, we had plenty of free time. The next week, we cleared twenty lots and had time to spare. Of course, you could no longer stand on one corner and see the other three, but it was looking country.

The Cook twins from Clover were on our crew and took it upon themselves to teach us about life. Being older and wiser, they felt that they owed it to us young bucks to share their knowledge.

This included flora and fauna and irritated us to no end. Jack and Gary were the chainsaw operators and were always two or three lots ahead of the rest of us. We were all pulling brush to the road to be burnt and they were off chasing rabbits or squirrels or birds or something.

At lunchtime, as usual, Mr. Cook started in scolding them for trying to harm God's creatures. Jack told him to mind his own business and stop butting in where he wasn't wanted.

For some unknown reason, this reprimand upset Mr. Cook and he turned his back on us and quietly finished his lunch. He was playing absentmindedly with a small stick, when a Cardinal landed not fifteen feet away and started chirping.

The old man said "Why don't you just shut-up?" and flipped that stick at the bird. He caught it right square in the head and killed it dead as four o'clock.

Gary yelled "All right Cookie, good shot."

The rest just sat there dumbfounded. The old man had inadvertently drawn first blood. Something, Gary and Jack had been trying to do for weeks. He had to go home early that day, but from then on, there was a new respect for that sureshot.

Bobby Yon's house was already finished when we moved into Heritage and Mr. Cook was no longer with us. His age got the best of him. Every once in a while when things were quiet and we were all sitting around together, someone would bring up the bird story and we would all have a good laugh.

A lot of people were involved in getting River Hills Plantation ready and most are still around somewhere. Ask about, you may find someone who saved your favorite Dogwood or Cedar tree. We even moved a road ten feet to the left to miss a Curly Maple. Ask me, I'll show you where it happened. I can also show you where the great Bird Killing took place.

Thank You Captain Lyle

For Diane's birthday, we ate at the "Thing You Hit With a Stick", you know the Mexican place on "49". The food was delicious, the Margaritas were fantastic, order the medium size, and the fellowship was outstanding. There was something missing though. For years I ate in that same building and always heard yelling and screaming coming from the kitchen.

Of course I'm talking about Capt'n Lyles' Seafood House. For those of you from up North, it was a fishcamp. Dot and Lyle Ferguson ran it along with their children and anyone else careless enough to be there at opening time. The booths were all high backs, so the kids at the next table couldn't catch you unaware with a hushpuppy. They were also long, fishcamp goers were notorious for bringing the whole family, and they wanted to sit up to sixteen people together. That way everyone ordered something different and you shared what you had with the others.

Capt'n Lyles had the best tarter sauce in the world. Donnie, the swarthy lady's man of the children was in charge of mixing up the sauce. This was done in a five-gallon bucket by hand. It was always better when he hadn't lost a Band-Aid during mixing. Lyle Jr. was the assistant cook, helping his Dad turn out some of the best fish you ever tasted. Ray, the baby just kind of hung around and took care of the oddjobs. He also bussed tables when some of the help layed out, but not without a lot of scratching and clawing and yelling "Make Donnie do it, he never does anything".

The girls, Sandy and Phyllis waited tables and flirted with the menfolk to get better tips. I have to admit that I would have tipped either one anything they wanted.

Just about any night after nine o'clock, you could find the regulars at the front booth. We were all waiting for Donnie to get off, so we could go on the prowl. We always drank a pitcher of tea and usually finished off the leftover shrimp. I'm not sure why Dot put up with us, but she seemed to like the fact that we were there. On a good night she would even join us and tell a joke or two, even though she usually ruined the punch line and embarrassed Phyllis immensely.

The regulars included Snake, Cotton, Jerry, Willy, Danny, myself and others. On occasion, some of the girls from Clover would show up and the party really got out of hand. You could smell Capt'n Lyles' Bleu Cheese dressing all the way to Five Points and like good Scotch, it was an acquired taste. I loved it and have been looking for its equal ever since with no success. Gale Hines was at the community table one night when I ordered a salad with Bleu Cheese dressing. You could smell it coming from the kitchen. She asked, "How can you eat that?" I told her how you had to hold your nose and make sure the dressing got on just the right part of your tongue to get all the flavor. I then offered her a bite. She stuck her fork into what she thought was a clean piece of lettuce and popped it into her mouth. That clean piece of lettuce was a large hunk of pure cheese. She gagged for thirty minutes and swore she would never trust me again. To this day, I don't think she does.

That front booth was the beginning of some great adventures. After closing one night we all rode to Rock Hill to buy some grass. A car followed us most of the way back home and we sifted that grass out the windows a little at a time until it was all gone, that's when the car turned off. I still think we were had anyway, that stuff looked a lot like fescue.

Taking the waitresses home was the main reason for hanging around. Usually this involved a side trip to White Wife Hollow, or Spook Road or some other aptly named out of the way place. Two or three of the guys would leave early to make sure that a spook would show up and the rest of us always rode together. One night Danny and Willy went to Spook Road and waited for us. When we arrived, Snake wouldn't get out of the car; he sat in the back seat with his head stuffed into a pillow. We got out on the bridge and told the tale about the floating head and watched the water below. We still hadn't seen Danny or Willy and were beginning to think they had gone home. We turned to get back in the car and it was gone. The running water had masked the sound as they drove away and left us. As we started up the road, Danny ran out of the weeds and scared the Dickens out of all of us. Jean got tickled and started snorting. When we asked her what was wrong, she said "SNORT...I wet my pants...SNORT"

Shortly after that, some of the guys started dating some of the girls and we all knew the good days were over. It's hard to pull a joke on someone you are trying to impress.

We still went back and shared tales at the big table, but the adventures stopped and people went their separate ways.

Kids today could use a community table and could use some good friends like the Ferguson's to look after them. As I raise my Margarita, "Here's to you, Dot and Lyle, wherever you are."

Mike A. Marr, Sr.

Strange Depressions in The Earth

I recently tried to get in touch with a friend of mine and was told that he had checked out on a top secret Government project. I left my name and the message that if I could help in any way to call me. When I got home, I had a strange message on my answering machine. It said, "Mike, thanks for your offer. On Friday, a few of us will be doing surveillance of some small depressions in the Earth. These depressions show up in groups of 18 and are about four inches in diameter. If you still feel the need to help, it would be most appreciated. These holes are located at Carolina's Country Club and tee time is 10:40. See you then."

These sinkholes seem to be everywhere today. In small towns, large cities and even in the country. When I was growing up in Lake Wylie, there were few golf courses around. The only one my friends and I were familiar with was at the Country Club in Gastonia. We didn't get to play but we did get to walk the course with other players, of course we had to carry their bags.

As many of you know, I was there at the birth of River Hills Plantation and got to see landscape change as the golf course was literally carved out of the hills. When it was completed in the early '70s, the employees were allowed to play. Many of us did, every afternoon. Some of us became quite good at the game and continued playing long after our stint at River Hills. There were those, however, who had a hard time distinguishing between golf and softball. The swings seemed similar, but the results were usually disastrous.

There is a tree on the 5th hole that still has the scars from a five iron swung by Carl Harrison. Carl found his ball under the brush beneath the tree and swore he had a decent shot, he also didn't need any additional strokes. With a mighty swing, the ball dribbled into the fairway. The five iron wrapped around the tree and broke.

Carl stood there stunned, looking at his club and with a seriousness unusual in his voice said, "You know, these things are made out of really thin metal." I think Carl ended up with a twelve on that hole.

Jimmy Burton played with us one day. He lost nineteen balls on eighteen holes and was borrowing from all of us before we finished. Back then there were very few houses on the course and the woods were very thick, but I think he could have found some of them.

On hole # 8, some sadist put a pond right in front of the tee box. There is no better place on Earth to top a ball than on Hole # 8 at River Hills Plantation. I watched Wayne Ballenger do it three times, before clearing the pond. On his fourth tee shot, the ball hit the water and skipped four times, before clearing the other side and heading toward the sand trap on the right. It never made it. The ball caught a tree and bounced back into the pond on the other side. We convinced Wayne to lay out on the other side, laying nine. I think he took a twelve on that hole.

Golf at River Hills has changed dramatically since those early days. I doubt if anyone plays in cutoff blue jeans anymore. The equipment is all new not thirty year old mismatched clubs. And no one pulls his shoes off to climb into # 8 pond to retrieve a ball like we did. You can stand on one foot and feel around on the mud and find a lot of balls, maybe enough for Burton to finish a round. Many things have changed, but no one ever had as much fun as those early foursomes on a late fall afternoon.

Mike A. Marr, Sr.

Oysters and Seagrass Baskets

Edisto Island is one of the prettiest little towns in South Carolina. I was down there last week for the first time in a long while. Nothing much has changed except for a few condos here and there. Years ago, we lived in Summerville and Edisto was our weekend retreat.

One weekend while Diane's sister and her husband were visiting we rode out to the island. On the way back the tide was out as we crossed one of the many marshes and I mentioned all the oysters just laying out there for the picking. Of course, Johnny had to disagree and was adamant that oysters came from deep out in the ocean. I slammed on brakes and pulled to the side of the road. I removed my shoes and across the mud I went to get a small cluster. I would do anything to win an argument. When I got back the trunk was open and Johnny was standing there with a paper sack. "Since you are already muddy", he said, "Why not get a whole bag full."

I sloshed back into the muck and filled the bag. That night we had one of the best oyster roasts ever. Things were going really well until a small crab crawled out of Johnny's oyster. He didn't eat anymore and I'm pretty sure he wasted the ones he had already eaten.

Daddy used to tell the story about how he and Uncle Elmer singled-handedly built the bridge at Georgetown. One night they were sitting around with a group of locals eating oysters. One of their buddies had a pile shucked in front of him and asked Elmer if he wanted one. Uncle Elmer never being one to turn down food said yes. The fellow hooked one on his fork and fed it to my uncle.

He asked, "Got that'un down?"

Uncle Elmer smiled and grunted "Uh-huh."

The fellow hooked another one and the process repeated itself until the pile had disappeared. With the last one the man said again, "Got that'un down?" When Uncle Elmer assured him that he had swallowed it, he continued, "I had them all down one time myself but they wouldn't stay." I think Uncle Elmer wasted his, too.

Enough about oysters and Edisto, I want to tell you about a lady I met on the way from Edisto to Elizabeth City. She was one of the most savvy business people I have ever run into and believe me I have met a few. Within two minutes she knew how much money I had in my pocket, that I didn't carry a checkbook, and that if needs arose I had an ATM card that could be used to get more cash. Marie Rouse's business is strictly cash or check and she is very good at what she does. You will always find her along the side of the road in the town of Mt Pleasant.

Before you get the wrong impression, let me explain that I don't usually stop for women plying their trade on roadsides but I was looking for something in particular that day and Marie looked like she could fill the bill. She had every size and shape imaginable and they were all put together extremely well.

She had one in particular that she thought I would really be interested in especially when she found out it was for my wife and that it was not a special occasion. I told her how nice it was but there was another one I had my eye on and that was the one I wanted to talk about. She had slipped up and given me the price early in our dickering and by now had forgotten how much she had said or was sure that I had forgotten. The new price matched my money clip exactly. I argued that the price was lower before and her niece corrected her and backed me up. She gave me one of those hurt looks and said, "I gwana hafta fire that girl".

As I said before Marie knew how much money I had and was bound and determined to separate me from it. She came up with a deal that I couldn't turn down and I drove away with just enough cash to buy lunch.

By the way, Diane loved both sweetgrass baskets and she will never know how much they cost me. Value, after all, is in the eye of the purchaser and I got my money's worth just from meeting Marie. The baskets were only an added benefit.

Mike A. Marr, Sr.

Shagging in New Bern

The waves lapped gently against the bulkhead in rhythm to the beach music in the background. Diane and I sat on the park bench and watched the boats rock slowly back and forth. The lights from across the river shimmering on the rippled surface gave a romantic glow to the evening. Off to the left, fishermen in the Waterfront Park were still trying to catch that last nibble before calling it a day. Below us the lights were going out on the many yachts travelling from the god-forsaken North Country to beautiful Miami. Among them, a 76' Hatteras whose dinghy wouldn't fit under the new bridge. There was also a 1946 Chris Craft with the original wood still in tact. Each slip held more money than I make in ten years.

Lake Wylie? No, we were far from Lake Wylie. The place was New Bern, NC and we were there for a shag workshop. Ed and Deb Farris fell in love with the place and I wasn't sure we would get them to come back home. There were folks from all over the southeast including Gastonia, Rock Hill and Charlotte enjoying the company of fellow shaggers. Kathy St. Clair cornered me and told me how much she enjoyed these columns and I thought a comparison of our waterway and their waterway was in order.

After a long and relaxing weekend we left New Bern which is about six and a half-hours from Charlotte. It took us over ten hours to get home. We drove out to the little town of Oriental on the Pamlico Sound and watched the sailboats. The harbor held more boats than there were houses in the town. From Oriental we caught the ferry at Minnesott Beach and crossed over to the back road into Beaufort. We hit all the nautical shops and acted like real tourist. Lunch was on the water and I even talked Diane into eating a shrimp burger. The rest of the trip home was uneventful and I caught a nap down around Lumberton.

When we finally crossed the Buster Boyd Bridge, I looked out over the water and was shocked at the number of motorboats still zooming around. Darting in and out between them were those little whiney sounding jetskis. I wondered how any of them were having any fun at all when they had to be on constant guard against idiots.

The most noticeable difference between downeast and Lake Wylie was the lack of jetskis. Everyone seemed to prefer using the wind as a mode of transportation. Kids who would normally be riding Seadoos were riding windsurfers instead. The waterways were quiet and peaceful and unstressed. The people were quiet and peaceful and unstressed. Like Ed and Deb I didn't want to come home either.

In the '70s, Mrs. Carr from Fairway Ridge would take her little Sunfish out on the lake every morning. She once told me that the best thing that could happen to Lake Wylie would be for someone to put a metal net one-foot beneath the surface. That way everyone would have to sail and everyone would have to get along. After spending time downeast I tend to agree with that lady.

Mike A. Marr, Sr.

Mint Juleps

When you are in the middle of a long drawn out story and a southern listener states, "I declare", they won't. It is just their way of saying "What you are telling is interesting, but I personally couldn't care less."

One of the important lessons taught to all southerners is not to offend others, but as in football, the best offense is sometimes a good defense. Over time we have developed certain words and phrases to use as defense mechanisms. Listed below are terms southerners use and the true meaning of those terms.

1. "Ya don't say" = "I really wish you wouldn't say"
2. "Ah, really" = "I don't believe a word you have said"
3. "Landsakes" = "I would give you half of my holdings if you would just go away." Can also be stated as "For Heavensake" or "Mercysake"
4. "Well I'll be" = "I heard this bit of gossip yesterday and knew where you were going with it"
5. "You never know" = "I've known that for years. Are you just now finding out?"
6. "Do tell" = "Don't tell, haven't you said enough?"
7. "Ya Think?" = "Are you really that gullible?"
8. "Imagine that" = "I can't, how can you?"
9. "Eheheheheh" (this is the schwa sound as a in ago) = "Let me get this lie straight before I put it on the table."

Some phrases are used to soften the blow when you are about to say something bad about someone. You can say anything you would like as long as you add the phrase, "Bless their little heart." It is a rule that no offense can be inferred when using this little gem.

Examples:

"Did you see Brenda's wedding dress? I swear it made her look pregnant. Bless her little heart."

"Bless his little heart, that Tommy is dumber than a rock."

There is one term that we only use on very special occasions. It is best explained by listening in as two young women on the veranda of a large antebellum home try to get to know each other. One is sipping a mint-julep while the other has a southern comfort in her hand.

Mint-Julep says, "See that swimming pool down there? My daddy gave me that for my sixteenth birthday in hopes that I would someday be an Olympic swimmer."

Miss comfort answers, "That's nice."

Mint-julep continues, "See those tennis courts beyond the daylillies? My daddy had those built for me when I had a such a crush on that cute Boris Becker."

Miss comfort answers, "That's nice."

Mint julep takes another sip, pulls her glasses down to the end of her nose so she can see over them and continues, "See that red Mercedes convertible in front of the stables? My daddy gave me that on my eighteenth birthday just because I like red."

Miss Comfort says, "That's nice."

Now, very much perturbed, Mint julep says, "Look here, girl, I have been telling you my life story and all you can say is that's nice. Aren't you the least impressed? What do you mean, that's nice."

The other young woman slowly and deliberately sets her drink on the table and begins, "Unlike some folk's ancestors my great great granddaddy wore a gray uniform during the recent unpleasantness with the north. My great granddaddy lost all his holdings to carpetbaggers when they came south, therefore my daddy was unable to bestow material items upon me. He did however teach me the proper way to handle obnoxious people in a genteel manner. He taught me to say, that's nice, instead of telling you where you can stuff that swimming pool, tennis court and red Mercedes convertible."

Mint julep looks stunned and says, "I declare."

Mike A. Marr, Sr.

On The Lake

I'm upstairs and the rain is falling hard. It is very hard to concentrate because my eyes are closing. What is it about a rainy day that makes you want to sleep? Everyone has been complaining about the drought but if you look out my window right now you would think they were crazy. The drive is underwater, the grass is underwater and as I look across the field my tomato plants are underwater. This seems to be a perfect day to reminisce.

As I crossed the bridge the other morning, I noticed that there were not many boaters out there on the water. It wasn't exactly glassy but it was smoother than I have seen it in quite a while. My mind drifted back to the days when Mill Creek and upper Crowder's Creek were always as smooth as a mirror. We would ski on those back coves and it was as close as we could get to flying.

The Wootens lived on Mill Creek and since Snake was dating Judy we had access to one of the finest ski boats on Lake Wylie. In the late afternoon Mr. Wooten would fire her up and away we would go. Of course, he did have a mean streak and couldn't stand smooth water so he would start doing figure eights. The chop would get so high that you spent most of your time just trying to stay up. With the close turns there was no way to stay in the wake and you eventually became airborne flying from one crest to the next until your legs finally gave way and you went down. As he helped you into the boat he always said the same thing, "I thought you could ski."

Woody Wooten was a salesman. Snake told me once that Woody had actually convinced him to eat a whole bowl of candy. A type of candy that Snake didn't like. His salesmanship came into play one day as we were all going to visit their relatives in Belmont, up above the Hot Hole. It was a long trip so he talked me into using the banana skis because they wouldn't be as hard on my knees. Banana skis for the uninitiated are very wide and very flat and you feel every bump in the water. Coming up Mill Creek wasn't too bad and Snake was beside me cutting in and out of the wake. I should have known something was up by the silly grin on his face. I moved out of the wake and the smooth water was skiing through butter, the big skis were easy to maneuver and I was

Hero of Bullfrog Hill

looking forward to the rest of the ride. I seldom skied doubles anymore but Woody had said it would be easier.

That's when we caught the main channel which was full of boats of every size and type. I think some of those waves had whitecaps. I went as far as I could before the slapping of the skis on the hard water got the best of me and down I went. Woody pulled the boat around and as always said, "I thought you could ski". That evil smile was on his face and Snake was laughing out loud. I looked up at him and said, "Just drive the boat".

By the time we reached the Hot Hole, I had fallen ten or more times and it wasn't funny anymore but being hardheaded I wouldn't give up. We used the slaloms coming home and I did much better even though my calves were as tight as banjo strings. I walked funny for the next few days. I never trusted Woody after that trip.

The rain is falling harder now and I remember skiing a few times in rainy weather. It is hard to believe that those little drops of water could hurt so much. Skiing in rain feels like someone is sticking little needles in every part of your body. Today, instead of going skiing, I think I'll grab a good book, open the window and take a long nap. I'm sure my legs will appreciate it.

Mike A. Marr, Sr.

Gambling Addiction

I have a gambling addiction. There, I've said it and now it is public knowledge. There are quite a few people in our community with this problem and I feel for each of them. My addiction, however, unlike theirs is not expensive, unless you count the lost time.

Gambling with money is something I don't understand. We went to Amelia Island several years ago and took the boat out past the twelve-mile limit, where gambling is legal. I put a quarter in one of the machines and didn't even get a piece of bubble gum out of it. That ended my gambling, I couldn't see any profitable purpose to it. Diane, I think, would have lost a large sum of money if she hadn't spent most of her time on the upper deck. I think she was counting fish, she kept looking over the side.

Pinball machines were my favorite as a young man in Lake Wylie. They were everywhere. Earl Moss's store, where the Roadhouse now stands was a haven for gamblers. We would stand around and cheer as someone would try to get the shiny steel ball to drop into the 24 pocket for four in a row. These machines are marvels of technology. The flashing lights and pictures of pretty girls were an invitation to spend a few nickels and a little time and just maybe hit the jackpot. Of course, all these machines had a warning in bold print that they were for entertainment only. YEAH!

I'm not picking on Earl, all the stores had them and all of them had their own personality. Some had racecars on the front screen, some had rockets, some airplanes, but all had scantily clad girls and all had the same number of holes and five balls that bounced around and ended up in one or the other of these holes. The trick was to get the balls into the right combination of holes. By adding more money you got bonuses which allowed the screen to shift and you could collect on different combinations. I never had enough skill to put too much money in them, but I did usually spend a quarter and get the first shift. I have seen people put as much as five dollars at a time in them. After shooting all the balls, they would shift the screen around and collect on three or more combinations. These guys were good and could get the bell to do exactly what they wanted it to do. By varying the tension on the plunger, they could start the ball out at differing speeds and control where it would go. There was a certain amount of skill involved in pinball and a certain amount of physics. Unlike the new video poker machines, you did have some control over your destiny, and the payoffs could be huge.

As I said, I have a gambling addiction. My addiction is FreeCell. It is a computer game that will take up two or three hours if you are not careful. The idea is to spread all fifty-two cards in eight columns. You have four free cells that you can move cards into until you find somewhere else to put them. You first free all your Aces, and then deuces and so on until you have arranged all the cards into the four separate suits. If you fill all the free cells you lose. It is real easy to push a button and play again and before you know it, you have wasted several hours.

I guess the people who play Video Poker have the same problem, with the exception that each push of the button cost them money, sometimes lunch money, sometimes rent money and I have even heard of people playing on borrowed money. I understand the compulsion to beat a machine. What I don't understand is the compulsion to lose money to do it. Wouldn't it be cheaper to buy a computer and play for free? Then, all you lose is the time you should have spent writing an article that doesn't make people mad.

Mike A. Marr, Sr.

A Little Quiet Time

I awoke the other morning and turned on the News like any other morning. I grabbed a cup of coffee form the kitchen, took the instant Cream of Wheat from the microwave and sat on the couch to get my first dose of the new day. I looked out the window and saw the first rays of sunlight coming through the trees and noticed the birds flying around the feeders. The heat wasn't running, the dryer wasn't buzzing and no cars were going by, so I turned the television off and just sat there. It suddenly dawned on me that what I missed most from my youth was "Quiet".

Farley and Spenser were lying in the flowerbed where I had spread the leaves form last fall's raking. The cats were on the deck rail preening themselves and the only movement was the birds. It was the kind of quiet you hear after a heavy snow and there just isn't enough of it anymore. I must have sat there like that for half an hour because when I sipped my coffee, it had gotten cold.

I remembered a time when life was always quiet, a time when you actually looked up when an airplane flew over. I remembered sitting on the front porch listening for the mailman, you knew the sound of his old car and could almost hear him slamming the Mauney's box shut. Shortly, he would round the corner and I would tear off down the hill and take the Weekly Reader from his hand. In the summer, our box was seldom opened.

When there was snow, you could count on hearing Junior Mauney's engine racing from the bottom of their drive where he inevitably got stuck. You could hear Agnes yelling, "Bobbeeee, Billeeee" and Aunt Stella calling, "Randeeeee", and knew that all three were down on Bullfrog Hill having the time of their lives.

On Saturdays, you could hear the sounds of a ballgame coming through the hollow from behind John Lee's beer joint, there was the cheering of the ladies and occasionally, the sound of a fight between the men when someone didn't agree with the call at home plate. As evening rolled around, you knew those sounds would turn into the constant blare of the old jukebox, which played long into the night.

After one ballgame, I remember sitting on the porch and hearing someone running through the cornfield beside the house.

We watched as he juked and jived from row to row and we jumped when the shot rang out and he fell in the driveway. An old pickup pulled up and several guys got out and loaded him in the back. A couple of them waved as they drove off.

The incident didn't make the six o'clock news that night so I don't know whether he died or not. Nothing, in the Lake Wylie area, made the news back then. We lived so far from Charlotte that it seemed like a foreign country to most of us, not that it doesn't now, but it has gotten a lot closer.

Another sound that seems so far away is rain pattering on the tin roof of the old Oakridge School house where I grew up. On hot summer nights, you could hear the rain coming across the open field and the steady rumbling of the tin made for the best sleep you have ever had.

The old house is gone now along with the quiet that surrounded life in it. You seldom hear the neighbors calling their kids for supper and you can't tell the mail lady's car from all the Gastonia traffic that has found the shortcut to Charlotte. Airplanes are now a constant drone in the sky and none of them know how to sky write anymore, they are just in a hurry to get people somewhere else.

John Lee is dead now and the old ball field is grown over with weeds. Although, I swear, sometimes late at night, you can still hear that old jukebox pounding out the beat or maybe it's just one of the many kids running up and down Oakridge these days with their stereo wide open.

It is still quiet on this Friday morning and the Cardinals and finches are still feeding. The dogs have left the flowerbed and gone in search of a squirrel to chase and the cats are fighting over a dead field mouse. Strangely, there is very little traffic. Maybe I'll just sit here and listen for the mail lady. Hopefully, she will have my Weekly Reader.

Mike A. Marr, Sr.

Shag

With summer just around the corner, everyone is thinking of the "Beach". There are beaches in Florida, Virginia, North Carolina and I assume in places like California, but here, there is only one "Beach". The Grandstrand stretches from the North Carolina line to Georgetown, but the "Beach" is located in OD, that's Ocean Drive for those of you not familiar with the state dance. OD is the Mecca of all the shaggers, and at least one trip to SOS is mandatory.

We were hanging out at the "Windmill" not long ago, when a young lady at the bar asked if we did that new fangled Shag, the one where your feet move around a lot. I smiled and told her we did the same Shag that people had been doing in Lake Wylie for the last twenty years or so. About that time, Summy cranked up something by Solomon Burke, and Diane and I hit the dance floor and our feet moved around a lot. The reason we were there was because the York shag club meets at the Windmill, the first Saturday night of each month. Summy plays the tunes and everyone has a great time.

Diane had been nagging me for the past year or two to take Shag lessons, again. On Tuesday nights, Deb and Ed Ferris are teaching remedial Shag and we signed up I was talking with one of the couples in the beginner's class and mentioned the term, remedial. The young man said, "You mean Intermediate, don't you?" I told him "No, I mean remedial, we didn't get it the first time."

You have to understand we've been taking lessons for years. The problem is that we don't put those lessons to use often enough and when we have opportunity to dance, we end up doing the basic step, over and over. We have taken lessons from some of the best dancers in the Carolinas, Charlie and Becky (sticklers for little details), Darrel and Belinda (the Sugarfooters) Barry and Mitzi (male domination rules) and now with Ed and Deb (it doesn't matter as long as you look good).

The first Shag lessons I can remember; were given at old barn out on Turkey Road in the late sixties or early seventies. Jerry and Ginger brought those steps to the Meadowbrook, a club that was located at the corner of Highway 557 and Bethel School Road. Meadowbrook is gone now, but a lot of good Shaggers got their start right here in Lake Wylie. Those dancers moved on to Gastonia, Lancaster, Rock Hill and places unknown. Lessons have been given at the Old River Rat, Goodtimes and many homes in the area where the furniture has been moved back and the stereo blares "Myrtle Beach Days".

Beach Music and the Shag are a generation bender. Our children enjoy the same music we do and even do the same steps. Rob and Ginger have taken lessons with us and Arnie is in our remedial Shag class now. Mothers dance with Sons, Fathers dance with Daughters and everyone has a great time. The son of one couple in the beginner's class plays with the Ember's and they are taking lessons for the first time to surprise him. There are Junior Shaggers, Senior Shaggers and Middle Aged Shaggers and anyone of either group can dance with anyone else.

So, in answer to that young lady's question, "Yes, we do that new fangled Shag, where your feet move a lot. We've been doing it for as long as there has been Beach music". My only suggestions to her is grab a partner, break out your Weejuns and learn a few steps, you'll never regret it. For the rest of you, come on down to the Windmill and become a part of a Lake Wylie tradition that has spread throughout the Upstate. See you at the Beach.

Mike A. Marr, Sr.

Mister Duck

We were drunk, not commode hugging, knee crawling drunk but that sweet teenage tipsy kind of drunk, where everything becomes hilariously funny. We were only thirteen but it was still legal, I think, because we really hadn[1]t imbibed any alcohol. We had just smelled the fumes for several hours.

Duck Alexander had decided to grow grapes and when the grapes were ripe, he contacted the one man who knew more about alcoholic beverages than anyone else in the community, Claud Marr, my Dad. They picked the grapes and fermented them in fifty-five gallon barrels until they were ready to be poured up. That was where Jerry and I came in. We were hired to pour up the wine into gallon jugs. It was late fall and cold outside so we had a fire going in the old shop behind Mr. Duck's house, a tight little shop that held in heat and fumes. It wasn't too bad when the barrels were full, but as you neared the bottom you had to lean way over into the barrel to get a dipper full. You also got a snoot full of the most potent fumes in the world. By late afternoon we were plain silly and by the next morning we had the worst hangovers of our young lives.

That was my first job for Marshal B Alexander, but like most kids growing up here, it wouldn't be the last. I started working in the shop after school everyday when I was in the tenth grade. I mostly picked up and delivered lawn and garden tractors but I also learned how to work on them, how to tune the engines, sharpen the blades, adjust the belts and literally make a piece of junk into a high-powered lawn mowing machine. I also became confident enough to replace the valves in the old '55 Chevy I was driving. Those days in that old shop were some of the best learning experiences of my life.

Duck had come to Lake Wylie before I was born, had married a local girl and started a family. I learned a lot from him and a lot about him you couldn't help it, he talked constantly. He sold Allis-Chalmers tractors and someone once said he could talk a prospect into buying anything and then talk him out of it just as quickly. The man loved tractors and farming and probably should have lived in Nebraska or somewhere where farming was a way of life.

Duck drove the bus during the forties, that's right, there was bus service to Charlotte back in those days and he delivered local people to the Shell Plant to make weapons for WW2. His first shop was behind his house where we got drunk on wine fumes and then later he built the shop at the corner where Carolina Sales is today.

He was the first fire chief and was instrumental in the development of Bethel Volunteer Fire Department. Having the shop next door, he was able to keep the old trucks running and supply gas and oil. Some of those old trucks used a lot of oil. He also kept every car in the neighborhood running and in the spring the parking lot looked like a junkyard for old lawnmowers. Almost every kid around got to work on those mowers at one time or another. If you needed a job you went to see Duck. Even if he couldn't afford you he would find something for you to do.

In his later life he became a big part of the development of the new community of Lake Wylie. He served on the board of the first Chamber of Commerce and was a link between the locals and the gate community of River Hills. I guess that in his business he learned that the new people had car trouble too and that maybe they put their pants on the same way the rest of us did.

Duck died a few years ago, shortly after closing his business. He was tired and his hands were drawn with arthritis but he was still the best mechanic I had ever known. The remarkable thing about his last days was that he developed a sense of humor. I always remembered him as a very serious man but when I saw him in the hospital he reminded me of how Jerry and I were acting so many years before when we were pouring up wine. Everything was funny and he looked at everyone a little differently. He smiled.

I think he died a happy man and I will miss him. I'm not the only one, the whole community will miss him. My only regret is that God really did break the mold when Duck was born.

Mike A. Marr, Sr.

Death of an Inside Salesman

There's an old story about a man who was asked what he thought about Euthanasia. He replied " I think their parents should keep them home during the summer and make them work on the farm."

A friend of mine died today. He was unplugged. I would like to say he was a close friend, but I don't think he really was. People don't have close friends like they used to. With him it was hard to tell. He was a close friend with everyone who ever knew him. When he answered the phone, it was always a chipper "Bill Douglas", like he couldn't wait to solve your problem and that your problem was the most important thing in the world.

I don't like death, it's not fair, its inconsiderate, and at times it is slow and mean. My Dad died in 1990. He was unplugged. Dad had a stroke and was in the Hospital when he died. The doctors said he had brain damage and the life support was all that was keeping him alive. We agreed to pull the plug. It seemed to take forever for him to die. We sat around "Waiting for God".

Bill was a diabetic and had kidney problems. I had worked with him everyday for sometime and didn't notice that he was losing ground. Back in May, when I went into business for myself, I started seeing Bill once or twice a month and the changes in him were dramatic. I mentioned it to some of his co-workers, but they couldn't tell much difference from day to day.

Bill's eyesight was the first thing to go. We played Company golf together, Captain's Choice, and Bill would stride up to the tee, line up his shot, and take a good swing. He would then stare down the middle of the fairway and watch for his ball. Of course, he had either sliced it badly or dribbled it off the tee. Someone would always say "Bill, I think it went a little to the right". Bill would reply "After they go out there about 200 yards, I lose them". No one had ever seen Bill hit one 200 yards, but nothing was said. When we got near, we would kick it back into the fairway, if we could find it. I guess Bill had friends everywhere.

Bill worked for a guy named Roger, the greatest boss in the world to hear Bill tell it. No one else in the office would work for Roger, so they got along just fine. Roger would scream "Bill,

Hero of Bullfrog Hill

where did you put this", or "Bill, when are we going to get that out" and Bill would quietly say "Roger, you have to do so and so to it before I can send it out." Roger would then settle down and life would return to normal.

Bill's walls were covered with racecars and beautiful women. He loved to go to car shows and always shared his pictures when he returned. Bill never had a fancy showcar; he drove a pickup and had just gone through a divorce. I guess he still had dreams though.

My dog died, when I was a kid. It broke my heart because that dog never bothered anyone. I missed school the next day, but Mama wrote an excuse saying that I was sick. When I asked her why she would lie to the school, she said "Heartache is the worst kind of sickness, I didn't lie".

Well, I've got that old sickness once again and may need an excuse for tomorrow. You have all seen the Budweiser commercial, where the guy says, "I Love You Man", I honestly wish I had told Bill Douglas, "I Love You, Man!"

As for the Youth in Asia, let them play, life is too short to worry about them.

Mike A. Marr, Sr.

Waiting for God

Waiting for God can be an aggravating and tiring experience. My mother is in the hospital again for the second time in as many months. Her Systems are slowly but surely shutting down. Her lungs have breathed all the air they care to breathe, her heart has pumped all the blood it cares to pump and her kidneys have filtered all the water they care to filter. There doesn't seem to be anything specific wrong with her, just a lot of small things. If she were a car it would be time to trade it in on a new one before the old one nickel and dimes you to death.

Sometimes, instead of trading an old car in you just throw it away. I feel that we are now doing the same thing with our old people. I have been watching the new rest home rising from the red mud beside the Pantry and wondering how many of the future residents will be throwaways. People who were once useful and productive citizens of their neighborhoods who have slowed down a pace or two and can't keep up with today's technological advances. People, who if given a chance, would tell you about the first time they saw an airplane or the first refrigerator they owned or the first time they ever used a telephone and maybe some would even tell you about their first experience with indoor plumbing.

People like my mother are bypassed by the times. Mom tried to live by herself after my dad died and did quite well for several years. She lost most of her sight a few years ago and it kept her from doing the things she liked to do, like crocheting, knitting, gardening and even cooking. She was one of those people who put a seven course meal on the table for fifteen people in about thirty minutes and not even think about the fact that she didn't know fifteen people were going to show up hungry.

It became apparent two years ago that she wouldn't be able to care for herself much longer and my older sister took her home to look after her. Why is it always the sisters who get elected to be caregivers especially with mothers? I suppose that mothers don't want to burden their sons with their problems but they think nothing of burdening their daughters and sons-in-law. She lived with Clare for a while and everyone was happy except Clara, her

Hero of Bullfrog Hill

husband Ken and Mom. The next thing I knew Mom was back at home by herself and quasi-living a normal life.

She sat a lot and looked out the window though she couldn't see very much. I guess she was just waiting for someone to come by and say hello. I didn't go by there as often as I should have and I don't think anyone else did either. I can only wonder what she was thinking about the children she raised and the friends she made during the important time of her life. Or maybe she just sat there not thinking anything at all, that would be easier on the rest of us if it were true, but I have to believe that her mind was still intact and she had the same needs and desires for companionship that other people have. I apologize for not sharing as much time with her as I could have and I apologize for everyone else who has parents that they avoid. It just seems to be the way of the world today.

We put Mom in a rest home a few weeks ago. It was after a hospital visit for a stroke that took away her ability to swallow properly. We told her that she was going there for rehabilitation knowing all the time that she would never leave that place. Every visit included a conversation about how she was improving and would soon be going home. I would just nod and listen not able to tell her that she would never see her hilltop again. She had told me when she left Clare's that she was going home to die Maybe we should have let her.

She has now lost even the rest home. We were informed that she would probably never leave the hospital. So, we visit loyally and try to carry on a conversation and watch this woman we love slowly disappearing. We all sit around waiting for God.

Mike A. Marr, Sr.

Affairs of The Heart

St. Valentine was not as sadistic as we have made him out to be. If he were, he would never have made sainthood.

How can women say, "I love you" and make it sound like a question? Do they really need that much reinforcement? After all when a man says, "I love you" once, he means it, he doesn't want to go around repeating himself all the time. If the situation changes, I'm sure he will let his lady know. Until that time, what he says stands. It is hard enough for us to say it the first time, please be happy with what you have.

When I was in the first grade at Dear Old Bethel, a girl kissed me. It didn't make the headlines because it happened before sexual harassment became a household word. Besides, I kind of enjoyed it. Back then, Valentine's Day was a big event, all holidays were a big event. We were just learning that some days were more special than others. We were also learning that some people were more special than others. That young lady and I became sweethearts, a word not used much anymore. We sat together at assembly and played together during recess. I would tell her how pretty her hair was and she would comment on the dirt under my fingernails. She once told me that flesh colored fingernail polish would cover it up, it had been there for six years.

In February, the school chose a King and Queen for each class by counting the pennies collected in a jar with each couples picture on it. Therefore, it was not a popularity contest, it was a monetary contest. Every student could vote as many times as they liked by putting their ice-cream money in one of the jars. Alexis and I won and I have never been so embarrassed, remember I was only seven. Wonder what became of all that money?

Every year, on Valentine's Day, all the kids would show up at school with a grocery bag full of little envelopes. Each envelope had the name of a fellow classmate on the outside and a sweet sentiment on the inside. The trick was to balance them out between the boys and girls so that you never really ask a guy to be your Valentine. This sometimes required striking through mushy words and rewriting something more appropriate. Heart shaped pouches with each child's name were hung around the classroom. Each person put Valentines into these pouches, so no personal contact was required. You never knew, until you got home, which of the girls had a crush on you, that way you didn't blush in front of the guys. It was also a dangerous practice, sometimes the wrong girl got the wrong idea.

In High School, the teachers became more interested in good grades, than in matchmaking and Valentine's Day took a back burner. Cards were still passed but not in an organized manner. If you got a card, it usually meant that someone was really interested in you and you had better be careful, you might fall in love.

1969 was the Valentine's Day, of which I have the fondest memories. Diane and I had been to a dance at the Optimist Club in Clover. These dances were arranged to keep young people out of trouble. They usually involved the guys standing together talking man talk and silently wishing they had the nerve to ask a girl to dance, and the girls running to restroom every five minutes to adjust their garter belts which they weren't accustomed to wearing.

It started snowing around nine o'clock and everyone stood outside and watched. Ten minutes later, we realized the snow was sticking and the party broke up as everyone headed for home. The closer we got to Bethany, the harder the snow fell. I was scared as driving was becoming more and more treacherous. Diane kept sliding closer and closer and before long was really beginning to crowd me. I slowed the car and looked at her, "Aren't you scared?" I asked? She had the strangest smile on her face as she shook her head "no" and I knew I was in real trouble. This good-looking woman trusted me explicitly and my life was never the same after that night. I remember telling her as I dropped her off at home "I love you", but for some unknown reason, she still occasionally ask, "I love you?"

Mike A. Marr, Sr.

Vacation

Ah. Summer is finally here, the ultimate TG IF. If you're anything like us, you are preparing for *vacation*. Vacation is the time to restore our batteries, renew friendships with our families, and get away from it all for a while.

This is the one time each year when we all wish a part of our life away. When Diane flipped her calendar, she exclaimed "Only two more weeks after this week and we'll be on vacation." Rocky asked "Does that sound better than three weeks?" She frowned and told him to mind his own business.

Our vacations have become simple events as we have aged. We load up the car with towels, beach chairs, books by Nelson DeMille, Stuart Woods and Robert Parker and head out to Long Beach, North Carolina. There, we will lie in the sand and let the Sun slowly roast us to a golden brown. We eat, if we want to. We sleep when we want to. We do nothing, if we want to. The problem arises on Friday, when you realize that you have been doing nothing all week and are only half through. You really have to do nothing fast on Saturday just to catch up.

When I was growing up, vacation was the busiest time of the year. Daddy spent Monday getting the car ready, oil change, new points and plugs, and checking all the belts and hoses for wear. Then we were off to visit relatives and show off the new car and the new clothes and any thing else that might impress them. I never understood why it was important to visit people and then try to belittle them at the same time.

Daddy was one of those macho guys who bragged about how fast he could get to the mountains and how he knew all the shortcuts. We would leave home early in the morning and get to Tennessee by ten o'clock, but it was always late afternoon before we arrived at Granny's house. We stopped at every other house along the way because Daddy wanted to renew old friendships with people he hadn't seen in years. People, I didn't know, people I didn't care to know, people I wish he didn't know. When we finally pulled up at Granny's house, I thought we could just go to bed, but no, now we had to visit all the aunts and uncles living in the valley. Daddy would tell everyone how it only took two and a half hours to get there, even though by my watch, it had been closer to twelve.

As I got older, I started spending summers with my sister Sherill and missed the Mountain treks. I missed them like peasants in the Middle Ages missed the Black Plague. Sherill lived in Williamsburg and had great neighbors, mostly kids my age. I would catch the bus in Gastonia and make the eight-hour ride to Virginia. Those were some frightening trips for a twelve-year-old, especially when the Freedom Riders were moving on Washington. There was a lot of hate on those big Greyhounds, but I had grown up with Blacks and didn't understand that I was the outsider. I didn't know that they were supposed to ride in the back and always offered a seat when one asked, even when there was an empty seat right across the aisle. Those long trips are responsible for my love of Science Fiction. I spent many hours with A. E. Von Vogt and Isaac Asimov and never realized that I was in the middle of a history making Civil Rights event.

I was sixteen, before I discovered Myrtle Beach and learned that vacation meant doing nothing. I became quite adept at doing nothing rather quickly and have enjoyed it ever since. Thanks again go out to Captain Lyle and Miss Dot for inviting me to go with them.

Vacation does not necessarily mean a road trip, there are many things to do right here in Lake Wylie, if you are looking for something to do. You can swim, you can ski, you can visit friends or you can read a good book on the riverbank. As for me, I will be doing nothing at Long Beach and probably won't finish before Saturday.

Mike A. Marr, Sr.

Halloween Story 2000

Autumn has finally arrived in our little village and Halloween can not be far behind. Ghosts and Ghouls and Goblins will soon be roaming the streets looking for handouts from total strangers. With our history disappearing with each new development or shopping center, I feel it is time to chronicle some of the happenings of the past in this quaint little neighborhood.

I was raised in the old Oakridge School House. It was a huge cavernous building with ten-foot ceilings and a staircase that rose forever. If ghost ever visited Lake Wylie this house would have been their stopping place. I don't know how old the house was, but it should have finished settling years before we moved into it. Every night, though, you could hear the sounds of footsteps on the stairs, hear the doors creaking open, and the wind whistling around the window casings.

I was told ghost stories from the time I was very small and learned to take all of them with a grain of salt. You had to consider the source. My dad had spent his whole life making up stories to scare young'uns, but there always remained in the back of my mind the lingering thought that his spirits came from some substance.

I must admit that I had mixed feelings when we tore the old house down and moved into the new one. The school had been my tutor, my nanny and my friend. From the upstairs windows you could see the entire neighborhood. There were secret hiding places down in the cellar where even the best hide and seekers couldn't find you. There was also something sinister about the place that lay just out of reach. You knew something had happened there but no one would talk about it. "It's just your imagination", they'd say, or "Don't be foolish".

The year after the old school was gone my imagination got the best of me. Mom and Daddy were both working the third shift, which meant they left home around nine o'clock in the evening and didn't get back until the following morning. In those days people didn't worry about leaving children by themselves. Most of us were responsible enough to take care of any problem that arose and besides there was no media to tell people how to live their lives. I had not slept long when the sound roused me.

"Thunk". At first I thought I was dreaming, "thunk", but there it was again. "Thunk". It sounded like someone digging with a pickaxe up around the old school house site. The moon was shining full through my window and as I looked out she swung the mattock again, "thunk".

She wore a long full dress down to the ground and a bonnet that covered her face. The dress and hat were from the same piece of cloth and were probably the old women's Sunday clothes. She would dig and then look through the turned soil. I couldn't imagine what she was doing there or who she could possibly be. She didn't look dangerous so I jumped out of bed, pulled on my cutoff jeans and slipped out the back door.

She had her back to me as I approached and didn't hear me coming. I didn't want to scare her so I cleared my throat loudly and said, "Can I help you find something?" "Thunk", she continued digging. "Mam", I tried again, "Have you lost something here?" "Thunk", still no response.

Tickled that she was so deaf, I moved closer and touched her sleeve. "Mam?" this time she turned and stared with bright red eyes. No, there were no eyes, just empty sockets where her eyes had once been. She was nothing more than bones and before I could catch my breath she vanished into thin air.

I ran back to the house locked the door and crawled under the bed. I reached back and pulled the covers in around me. I did not sleep that night.

When the sun finally came up I heard the old pickup pull up the hill and I met my parents at the back door still shivering with fright. I could hardly talk but finally spit the whole story out in one breath. They looked at each other knowingly then my mother removed the small piece of cloth from my closed fist.

Daddy said, "Son, it's time we had a little talk".

Daddy sat down across from me at the old farmhouse table and said, "Son, what you probably saw last night was just a figment of your imagination but", he continued the smile creeping into his voice, "it could have been ol' Hazel."

I looked him in the eye and repeated, " ol' Hazel?"

"Hazel and Clem lived down by the river before the dam was built," he started. " They were a young married couple and were very happy. The river gave them fish and game and the rich bottomland provided vegetables and fruit. They had no need for anything else and shut the rest of the world out." He took a big swig of coffee from the mug Mom sat before him and continued, "They lived a long full life and seldom left the banks of the river. When Clem got older he became very sick and Hazel grew to detest him. She was constantly picking up after him and had to do all the work around the house and in the garden. Her life wasn't fun anymore."

"One fall day, while she was checking the trotline she noticed that the water was rising. It hadn't rained in days but the level was coming up quickly." He stopped, buttered a biscuit and spread a thick layer of honey on it.

"Where was I?" he asked.

"The river was rising", I said "They must have finished the dam and no one told them."

"That's right, the river was rising. Hazel ran as fast as her old legs would carry her back to Clem. Even though she hated him, he was all she had. The water was already coming in the front door when she got there. She ran inside, pulled Clem out of bed and told him to get dressed. Clem griped and complained as usual while Hazel grabbed what food she could. She half carried the old man up out of that valley and finally stopped right here. She built a fire and took a big pot out of her bag. She filled the pot with beans but couldn't find anything to use for seasoning." He stopped and ate two more buttered biscuits.

I asked, "Then what, what did she do then?"

"That's when she noticed that Clem wasn't moving. The stress had been too much for him and he had laid right there and died. Well, Clem had always taught Hazel to be resourceful and to use everything. Hazel being a little dazed by losing everything they owned, cut his toes and nose off and put them in the pot to flavor her beans. She then took a mattock chopped Clem up into little pieces and buried him."

He sipped his coffee and continued, "That night after supper, Hazel slept fitfully and was awakened by Clem walking around muttering, 'Who got my nose and my two big toes?' She jumped up so quickly that she tipped the whole pot of beans over into a ditch. 'Who got my nose and my two big toes?' Clem was gaining on her as she ran back toward the river. 'Who got my nose and my two big toes?' he grabbed her and drug her back to the campsite. He handed her the mattock and told her to find his parts so he could rest in peace. What they didn't know was that an old possum had come by and eaten the rest of those beans toes and all."

He pushed back from the table and got up, "They tell me that ol' Hazel spent the rest of her days digging the ground around her husband's dead body looking for his toes and nose."

I knew I had just been handed a line a mile long, so I got dressed and went on to school. I was still a little shaken and kept looking out the window before going to bed that night, but the ol' Hazel didn't come back. I felt pretty foolish and finally slipped off to sleep about ten o'clock.

When the clock struck twelve, I heard it and sat up in bed. It sounded more like a moan than actual words. I looked out but no one was digging, then I heard it again, "Who got my nose and my two big toes?"

"I'm dreaming", I thought as I sat there in bed. Daddy had just told me this great big yarn about Hazel and Clem and now I was hearing voices. I lay back down and pulled the covers up over my head. "Stupid story anyway," I said out loud.

"Who got my nose and my two big toes?" asked a deep eerie voice right outside my window. I jumped up and looked out again, I definitely wasn't dreaming this time. At the corner of the house I noticed movement but couldn't tell what it was. I was headed for the back door when I heard it creak open, "Who got my nose and my two big toes?" I knew now that this was no dream, dreams don't open doors.

I went into the closet and pulled the door almost closed behind me, someone or something was in the living room and was coming my way. The knob of the bedroom door slowly turned and the door crept open. A shape came through it and whispered those dreadful words again, "Who got my nose and my two big toes?" It walked slowly to the bed and pounced yelling, "YOU GOT 'EM".

I stepped out of the closet and said, "Hey Pop, What you doing home so early?"

Mike A. Marr, Sr.

These are the kind of incidents that used to occur during the Halloween season at our house. That was before we started protecting our children from everything that comes along. If someone did that today, they would be locked up for child abuse.

We also dressed for the occasion; you have never seen so many vampires, Frankenstein monsters and werewolves, as there were in Lake Wylie in the '50s and '60s, but not anymore. Now the only trick-or-treaters are Teletubbies or Barneys or Fairy princesses. People decorate trees with tiny plastic pumpkins and have orange and black streamers hanging from their porches. There are even special events planned whose soul purpose is to keep the kids off the street.

What happened to the good old days when it was more fun to scare someone than anything else you could do? I really believe that those scares prepared us for life. If we could live through Halloween, we could live through anything. That probably explains why there is so much stress in the world, children are not properly prepared to meet with the scary things in life. The first little bump in the road and they are frightened silly. There is no mommy and daddy to protect them.

Let's put the fun back in Halloween this year. You still have a few days to think up something crazy to do to your neighbor and to come up with a really original costume for your kids. Spend some quality time with them this year, go rent a classic horror movie and watch it with them. Better yet, invite the grandparents over and let them talk about their scariest Halloween costume.

Your kids may surprise you, they may want to dress up as Hazel and Clem.

The Best Christmas

Someone recently asked me what we do for Christmas down on the Lake I told them we do the same things everyone else does. We put up a tree in the house and decorate it with memorabilia from Christmas's past and scatter brightly colored packages underneath it. Then we go down to T-Bone's and watch the boat parade. Last years parade was the best ever A lot of thought went into some of those lights.

As for the tree, that is something that has to be sought out. Many November afternoons are spent in the woods looking for the perfect Christmas tree. When it is found and everyone is happy with the selection, we cut it down and drag it back to the house to be mounted in the tree stand. I have found that any tree that looks perfect in the woods will be at least two feet too tall for the spot you picked out to put it up. Also, the base will be two inches too big to fit into the tree stand. When these obstacles are overcome, you will notice the huge bare spot where you will swear there was a limb before. By turning the bare spot to the wall and filling in with the larger ornaments, a presentable tree can be had.

One Christmas, several years ago, My niece Joyce found the best tree of all time. It was just the right height, the right circumference, and the limbs were spaced about a foot apart a perfect circle around the tree. With pride, she cut it and took it home, not knowing that the little White Pine along with several of its brothers were being nursed and nurtured by her Uncle Ronnie. I'm not sure Ronnie ever knew what happened to that tree.

One winter when Ronnie's middle son, Jon was about five years old, they came to the house to search for a tree. Jon was at that independent age when no one could do anything for him He had to do it himself. I made the trek with them across the fields and through the woods and across the creeks with Ronnie constantly calling, "Come on baby", to which Jon cried out "I'm not no baby". We finally located a tree that suited them. Ronnie had the tree across one shoulder and the axe across the other and asked me to carry Jon. Jon, however would have none of that, he was going to walk all by himself. I said, "At least let me hold your finger", but Jon crossed his arms and trudged along with his lip stuck out.

Ronnie sped up and told me to come on. We stayed just far enough ahead that Jon could see us, but his short little legs couldn't catch up. Finally worn to a frazzle, he sat down and screamed at us, "Hold my fingoo, I' m a baby" I picked him up and he was asleep by the time we reached the house.

When I was seven or eight, I had already learned where to look for Mama's Christmas stash. She usually hid it in my Grandma's old icebox under the stairs. I checked it about once a week starting in late October. This had been a bad year and money was tight, but by mid-December, there was still nothing in the icebox. A family with six kids had moved in across the road and I knew Mama had been slipping them a little money now and then to help with groceries, but surely she wasn't going to skip presents for her own son, just so they could eat regularly. I had asked Santa for a gun set and a pump pellet rifle and was beginning to worry. Two days before Christmas, my worries were over. There in the bottom of the wardrobe was more stuff than I had ever imagined. There was a set of Paladin pistols with black holsters and a white chess knight in the center. There was also a Matt Dillon pistol set, a Rifleman sawed off rifle, and two more sets that I didn't have time to study. The funniest things were the three baby dolls in there. I didn't know what she planned to do with them and didn't much care, I was going to have the best Christmas ever and I couldn't wait.

As Christmas morning finally arrived, I was up at daybreak and ready to open presents. When I looked under the tree, I found the single action pump pellet rifle and a box of five hundred pellets. I was so happy, I completely forgot about the pistols and baby dolls and went out to kill me some birds for supper. As I looked across the road I froze in my tracks, there were those poor kids playing cowboys and Indians and tending to their baby dolls. I felt Mama's arm around my shoulder and brushed away a tear as she said "Pretty good Christmas, huh". All I could do was say, "Yeah, Mama, the best."

What No Santa

I don't think my Dad ever lied to me intentionally, even though he was known for his big tales. I never quite believed the one about how my parents got married. Daddy said he slipped up to my mother's window and whispered through the screen, "Hey, you want to get married?" To which she supposedly answered, "Lord Yes, Who is it?" Daddy did, however, do me a terrible injustice when I was only five years old. I'm not sure it was a lie, because he believed it. He told me there was no Santa Claus.

I don't remember why he told me but I do remember the look in his eyes. They were dull gray and the usual sparkle was gone. I was sitting on the old trundle bed in the back bedroom of the old Oakridge School house where I grew up. I was looking through the new Sears catalog that had just arrived and was amazed at all the toys. It was a month before Christmas and I was beginning to get antsy, the way little kids do at that time of year. Daddy came in and said point blank, "You know there is no real Santa Claus, don't you?" He'd had a bad year. Of course, at age five, I didn't believe him, and truthfully I still don't.

On Christmas Eve, there was nothing under the tree, when I went to bed, and I was quite worried. The next morning when I woke up I got out of bed I stumbled over something that hadn't been there the night before. Santa had left the one thing I had been hoping for, a shiny new Western Flyer bicycle with handle bar streamers and training wheels. I ran into the kitchen and Momma and Daddy were sitting there like nothing important had happened at all, but when he looked at me, those dull gray eyes were shiny light blue with just a tinge of a twinkle in the corner. "Merry Christmas" was all he said.

Santa comes into people's lives shortly after Thanksgiving. You can see him in their step, you can hear him in their voice, and you just know that twinkle in their eyes could be nothing less than the old Christmas spirit. Try as they may, people can't help getting caught up in the joy of the season. Everywhere you go people are friendlier, they open doors for you, they help you pick up the packages you drop and most importantly, they smile.

Mike A. Marr, Sr.

If you are having trouble getting in the mood for Christmas, this year, borrow your neighbor's two-year-old for an afternoon. Ask that child what Santa is bringing him and sit back and enjoy as he rattles off a list as long as his arm. Take him into the kitchen and bake sugar cookies and I'll guarantee he picks out one to leave for Santa. Load him in the car and drive him to McAdenville to see the lights and be prepared to be dazzled, not by the lights but by the smile on the child's face.

Now that your mood is slightly better, go by the Angel tree and pick out an angel. Spend a little more than you had planned on a gift for someone you will never meet. On Christmas morning, you won't be able to stop smiling as you imagine that child opening your present. Take the remainder of the sugar cookies you baked to an elder shut-in and watched their eyes light up, you might also bring some small gift. If you have children, let them go with you. If you give them the gift of giving early, it will stay with them the rest of their lives.

Sorry, Daddy, Santa does exist and is doing quite well in the minds and hearts of the people of Lake Wylie. May this truly be the best Christmas ever, and may you share your joy with everyone you meet. Merry Christmas.

About the Author

Mike Marr is a hopeless romantic who grew up loving everything about the South. He writes about the way things used to be before all the Yankees moved in and changed them to the way that they do it back home. Mike invented the word confraction that similar to contraction puts several words together and by twisting them around the tongue and holding them firmly between the cheek and gum creates a new word undecipherable above the Mason-Dixon Line. Squeet is a prime example that means let's go eat, something southerners do a lot. He lives in Clover, SC with his wife Diane, one Golden Retriever and some cats that leave paw prints on his pick up truck.

Printed in the United States
6451